Winner of the Leeds Book Award and Peters Book of the Year 2015
Nominated for the Carnegie Medal and the Branford Boase Award

'A really moving debut ... one for fans of Sarah Lean and Cathy Cassidy'
The Bookseller

'A real "feel good" read ... combines comedy with a cautionary note
... A new author to watch'
Picked as a NEW VOICE in the Guardian Independents supplement

'A beautifully written book with real insight ... A book to ponder over;
a book with a positive message; a book which shows people aren't
always what they seem' *Parents in Touch*

'... a special book that is destined to charm readers old and young'
We Love This Book

'Honestly, honestly, honestly, this story is just lovely. It's simply told
and easy to read but it's also beautifully written' *The Bookbag*

'Jam-packed with all the key elements of a perfect story ...
This is a novel that you simply won't want to put down'
Guardian Reader Review

'It's the best book I have ever read!'
Guardian Reader Review

'A touching story with many light-hearted moments, full of endearing
well-rounded characters' **Primary Times**

Also by Jane Elson

A Room Full of Chocolate

How to Fly with Broken Wings

Swimming to the Moon

Will You Catch Me?

A Room
Full of
Chocolate

JANE ELSON

Hodder
Children's
Books

HODDER CHILDREN'S BOOKS

First published in Great Britain in 2014 by Hodder Children's Books
This edition published in 2016 by Hodder and Stoughton

9 10

A CIP catalogue record for this book
is available from the British Library.

ISBN 978 1 444 91675 1

Typeset in Egyptian 505 BT Light by Avon DataSet Ltd,
Bidford-on-Avon, Warwickshire

Printed and bound by Clays Ltd, Elcograf S.p.A.

The paper and board used in this book
are made from wood from responsible sources

Hodder Children's Books
An imprint of Hachette Children's Group
Part of Hodder and Stoughton
Carmelite House
50 Victoria Embankment
London EC4Y 0DZ

An Hachette UK Company
www.hachette.co.uk

www.hachettechildrens.co.uk

For My Mum,

Jenny Elson, for her bravery

&

For these other courageous women

Rachel Wedderburn	Mary Thomas	Kathleen Cant
Bridget Espinosa	Jenni Evans	Ann Neaum
Emma Harding	Carey Hemsley	

& for all the Graces & Chloes out there

1

Mum found a lump under her arm on my tenth birthday.

I wrote this fact down in my Special Blue Book that I use for my stories and plays.

Dad had been shouting at her and had stormed out, and afterwards I heard her crying in the shower. I banged on the door.

'Mum, it's me, Grace. I need a wee desperate, like two-seconds-to-spare desperate.'

Mum let me in, all covered in soapy bubbles, but as I ran to the toilet I heard her gasp. It was only a small gasp but I heard it.

'What's wrong, Mum?' I said, flushing the chain and pulling the shower curtain aside so I could nick her soap to wash my hands.

'Nothing,' she snapped. 'I slipped.'

I turned the basin tap on and let the soap slip, slide in between my wet fingers and, wiping a hole in the steamed-up mirror, stared at my short brown scraggy hair. I hate it. My hair is my worst thing in the world. My eyes are brown too, just like my too-busy-for-me dad's. Mum – who is called Chloe, by the way – has twinkly sparkly blue eyes and I love her most in the whole wide world. She has lovely wavy brown hair. I wish with all my heart that my hair was like my mum's.

'Can I brush your hair out and blow dry it? Pleeeeease, Mum?' I asked, peeping through the shower curtain.

'No, not today. Go downstairs, it's tea time. We'll have your cake and candles.'

'Will Dad come back in time for me to blow out my candles?' I asked.

'No, my darling Grace, I don't think he will. Make your birthday wish,' and she put a soapy bubble on my nose.

But I didn't go downstairs. I crept to her bedroom door and listened as she phoned the doctor. I heard the words 'lump . . . arm . . . tomorrow . . .' trickle through the crack in the hinge.

I tiptoed downstairs and Googled 'lump' on the computer, and copied down what it said in my Special Blue Book.

Lump (noun): A piece of solid matter – a lump of coal.

Lump (verb): To tolerate a disagreeable situation. (For example, I have to lump Dad shouting at Mum.)

Lump (noun): A swelling under the skin caused by injury or disease.

Mum must have injured herself when she was dancing. She was always dancing, my mum. She would dance to anything – even the adverts and the signature tunes for *Coronation Street* and *Countdown*. She must have bumped herself on the furniture when she was waving her arms in the air, I told myself over and over again.

My eyes flicked back to the computer screen. I saw all the different reasons you might have a lump – how it could just be a cyst or something called an abscess. As I read down, scary words jumped out at me from the screen, so I shut my eyes tightly so I couldn't read them any more. Then I heard Mum's footsteps coming down the stairs so I switched off the computer.

As I closed my eyes and blew out my candles I wished with the whole of my heart for Mum's lump to disappear.

I couldn't eat my birthday cake after that. The purple icing choked me.

I wrote down in my Special Blue Book that:

I, Grace Wilson of 22 Manderly Road, Southgate, North London, feel in my heart that now I have reached double figures my life has changed forever.

It did. Mum went to the doctor's the next day and two weeks later she was sent to the hospital. She came back with one of those big smiles on her face, the sort that doesn't reach the eyes, and started to cook my best tea: pork chops, apple sauce and mash. I wasn't hungry.

The shouting behind closed doors got really loud after that. And then the dreams started. I wrote one down in my Special Blue Book, just as I woke up so that I wouldn't forget.

Mum turned into one gigantic fleshy lump while we were watching *Coronation Street* and her face completely disappeared. I was trying to phone my dad's office but the secretary on the end of the line kept saying, 'Mr Wilson is too busy,' over and over again and laughing.

My dad left soon after that, packed his bags of clothes and anger, then grabbed me and hugged me. He held me too tight and one of his shirt buttons was up my nose and I couldn't breathe and I was thinking *Please just let me go*, and then he did. My dad turned and walked down the path. He didn't look back once.

I thought Mum would cry, but she turned up

the music on the radio really loud and we danced round the house in every room until we flopped on the sofa, legs aching. We ate nearly a whole box of Quality Street, saving the strawberry creams till last. It was then she told me what I already knew. I put on my special I-don't-know-what-you're-talking-about face.

'Grace, I have something really important to tell you,' she began. 'I have a lump. Just a little lump.' She pointed to a place under her arm.

I didn't tell her that I'd heard her crying herself to sleep; that I'd listened at doors and to telephone conversations when she thought I was in bed, trying to piece together more words that trickled through the door hinge: country . . . clinic . . . rest . . . scared. I didn't tell her about my dreams.

'Grace, I am going to have to go into hospital to have a little operation to have the lump cut out,' she continued.

'It's OK, Mum,' I said. 'I'll look after you.' Then I said our special thing.

'Hug you, Mum.'

'Hug you more,' she said. 'The thing is, Grace, after they have taken the lump out I have to completely rest my arm. I won't be able to lift anything for a while. I won't be able to hoover, or peg up the washing, or drive you to tap dancing and clarinet, or your friends' houses, or do anything really. Isn't that boring?' And she laughed, but her eyes weren't laughing.

'It's OK, Mum – who cares about tap dancing and the stupid clarinet? I don't,' I said. 'I'll do the hoovering and the washing.'

'No, Grace, I won't be able to look after you.'

'I'll do the cooking. I'll do the dusting. I'll brush your hair,' and I raced up the stairs, two at a time, to get her hair brush and slid back down on my bottom. I started to brush Mum's curls, but she grabbed hold of both my wrists and pulled me so that I was standing in front of her.

'No, Grace! Stop! You're going to live with your Grandad Bradley on his farm in Yorkshire for a while.' Her hands were shaking.

For the first time since I learned to talk as a tiny baby, no words would come out. Mum hadn't talked to Grandad Bradley for eleven years. That was one year more than I had been on Planet Earth. I didn't even know my grandad.

I just stood there and looked at her with a hurricane in my head. Then I heard myself say like a baby: 'No, Mummy, please don't send me away. You can't send me to live with him. You said he'd been a miserable man ever since Granny Bradley danced off with her soldier man and left you when you were eight. You said Grandad Bradley was a miserable old goat. Please let me stay and look after you.'

'Sometimes,' said Mum, 'people come through unexpectedly.'

'Dad didn't,' I said.

'No, Dad didn't, he doesn't like hospitals,' she said, rolling her eyes and letting out a weird laugh that didn't tinkle but sounded like a donkey with tummy ache. 'Your dad is going to pick you up from school tomorrow to drive you up to Yorkshire.'

The tears started to bounce off my cheeks, making the last few chocolates soggy.

'Please, Mum, I'll pick all the things off the floor in my bedroom. I'll scrub all the floors. I'll do anything.'

'No, Grace,' she said. 'You leave tomorrow.

'Hug you,' she said, her voice cracking. And then again, 'Hug you?'

But 'Hug you more' jammed in my tonsils.

She reached under the sofa and brought out a box. 'I know I said you couldn't have a phone till you were eleven but these are special circumstances.' She nodded at me to open the box.

My new phone was purple and shiny and definitely one of my best things in the world, but the 'thank you' got stuck.

There was a knock on the door. It was our next-door neighbour, Mrs Johnson, whose sons were all grown up and gone away. Lovely Mrs Johnson who let me spend hours and hours in the tree house they were all too old to play in, writing in my Special Blue Book. She appeared in the doorway with a purple suitcase and a purple rucksack and purple sparkly purse.

'For you, Grace,' she said. 'For your exciting adventure.' They were the best bags ever but I had another major tonsil jam.

'I can look after myself,' I screamed instead, and ran up the stairs to my room, slamming the door so hard the house shook.

I kicked all the clothes on the floor out of the way and flung open my bedroom window. I leaned right out into the night air to look at Mrs Johnson's tree house. Just then a mangy fox scurried across our lawn and pushed his nose against the loose bits of wood in the fence which is my own top secret entrance, and wriggled through to Mrs Johnson's, disappearing into her rose garden. I leaned my Special Blue Book on the window sill, which is my best place, and wrote:

I am not a baby. I am ten years and five weeks and one day. Why won't Mum let me look after her? How can she send me away to live with a miserable old goat.

~~I HATE HER~~. I wish I could live by myself in the tree house.

I decided I was never going to come down from my bedroom, not ever. But I got hungry so I crept down the stairs to get a chocolate digestive and a glass of Fanta. I peeped through the front room door. Mrs Johnson was on the sofa, cradling Mum like a baby.

2

A VERY PRIVATE PART FROM MY SPECIAL BLUE BOOK
THAT I WILL LET YOU PEEP AT.

I am ignoring Dad and dipping my soggy chips in
ketchup at the 'Happy Diner – the Motorway's
Ultimate Eating Experience'. We have stopped here
after driving forever since Dad picked me up halfway
through my History lesson (on mean Henry the Eighth
chopping everyone's heads off). Can you believe Mum
actually made me go to school for the morning! She
said she had to be at the hospital for 9 o'clock and
Dad couldn't pick me up till 12.15, coz he had an
important meeting – blah blah blah – and it was best
if we treated this like any other day and I went to
school as normal.

HOW CAN THIS DAY BE NORMAL WHEN I AM BEING SENT TO LIVE WITH A MISERABLE OLD GOAT?

I am missing Maths, though, which is the only good thing in this whole tragedy. My class are doing rubbish sums while I am eating chips dipped in ketchup at the Happy Diner. Ha ha.

I just made a proper effort with my dad and everything. I even took my purple iPod out of my ears – the one he'd given me as a present when he came to pick me up and said in my best polite voice, 'So, Dad, when will I see you, please?'

But before he could answer, his phone rang. I shoved my iPod back in my ears. I won't bother talking to him again.

My new purple case is in the boot of Dad's car. I stayed up most of the night emptying everything from my bedroom floor into my case. I thought I would help Mum by packing and also, cleverly, tidying my room at the same time.

These are the things that Mum made me take out of my case this morning so she could force the lid shut:

Tap shoes

Clarinet

Music stand

Bedside lamp with purple glitter shade

Then we sat on my bed and she let me brush her curls for one last time. We walked hand in hand down the stairs and she hitched my new purple rucksack on to my shoulders before opening our front door.

My bones can still feel where Mum hugged me more and more and more like we were glued together forever. As I walked away from her down the path I knew she was trying not to cry and waving at me, waiting for me to turn round. But I didn't. I was frightened that if I did I would run and hold her and never ever ever let her go, so I just kept on walking.

I ran to catch up with Jessica and Kayla, dawdling ahead of me along the road to school, heads touching, whispering secrets, planning a sleepover without me. Jessica used to be my best friend till Kayla joined our class. Not that it matters now.

Dad is still on the phone but also mouthing at me to get in the car. I AM PRETENDING I CAN'T SEE HIM.

Ouch! I woke as my head hit the car window. Dad was bumping the car down a muddy farmyard track. At the end of the last bump was my Grandad Bradley.

I tumbled out of the car, cuddling my purple rucksack to my tummy tighter than a hot water bottle. Grandad Bradley was tall, with a big nose and a cross mouth, with the broadest of broad shoulders that seemed to hold up all the troubles and sadness in the world.

I could see that Grandad had my mum's eyes; it's just that his didn't twinkle. He had little tufts of grey hair sprouting from his head and the tops of his ears.

Grandad stared at me.

I stared back.

I won.

Dad and Grandad shook hands like strangers who didn't like each other.

Dad began, 'I'd better . . .' but his voice trailed off to nothing. He scuffed his shoe in the dirt with his hands in his pockets like a little boy, not my dad.

'You do that. You get going. Don't want to hit the traffic now, do you,' spat Grandad Bradley. Then he turned and looked at me and muttered under his breath, 'I'll do your duty for you, don't you worry. Grace'll be safe with me.'

'Bye, Grace,' said Dad. 'I've got to get back for a meeting,' and he pressed ten pounds into my hand. Then my dad just got back in his car and drove off. I wish with all my heart now that I had talked to him. He didn't look back. Ever.

I turned round and tried to smile at Grandad, but my mouth felt all wobbly.

Grandad looked down at me and tried to smile back, only I think it was a bit too much effort for his lips. It was like the world stood still as we waited for the words to come, then my head filled with squeals as a baby-pink pot-bellied pig ran over my foot.

Bang! The shabby door of a cottage across the farmyard flew open. As it crashed and splintered against the wall, butterfly flecks of old blue paint fluttered off in the breeze.

Out of the door ran a girl with wild black

curls and mud on her face. She wore a raggedy skirt of orange, yellow and green and a blue-and-indigo top with a red coat and wellies. The rainbow-girl shot across the yard, screaming, 'Claude, come back here!'

As she ran past me she pressed a tiny piece of paper into my hand. I screwed it tight in my fist and slipped it into my jeans pocket.

Grandad swooped the baby pig into his arms and gently quietened its squealing.

It was obvious that Claude the pig loved Grandad Bradley.

It was obvious that the rainbow-girl didn't.

She was agitated, hopping from one foot to the other.

'Thank you very much, Mr Bradley, sir, for catching Claude. Could I have my pig back now please, sir?'

Grandad Bradley totally ignored her and nuzzled Claude to his chest till he was completely calm. Then he looked up and said, 'I have told you time and time again not to run across the yard screaming like that.'

He passed the little pig back to the rainbow-girl, but as she grasped Claude she turned and gave me a tiny wink.

'Sorry, Mr Bradley, sir, it won't happen again.' Then she turned and walked back towards the door that had once been blue.

'Follow me,' Grandad grunted. 'I've put you in your mother's old room.' He lifted my case like it weighed no more than my iPod and strode off.

I stumbled on the mud bumps as I tried to keep up with him. I could hear what sounded like hundreds of cows mooing from a big long building and the sound of machinery pumping and sucking. A cockerel strutted past me, bossing the speckled hens that scuttled and scratched in the dirt at my feet.

As we reached the big old stone farmhouse Grandad opened the back door. A crazy bundle of golden fur hurtled itself at me, knocking me backwards on to my bottom. It started to lick my face.

'Give over, Lara, you soft lass,' shouted

Grandad to the golden retriever. Winded, I scrambled to my feet. A tear escaped and trickled down my chin, which was so annoying because, I promise you, I wasn't crying.

'You'll get used to her daft ways soon enough,' laughed Grandad. 'You're a town lass but you'll learn.'

'We have dogs in London you know,' I seethed, grabbing my rucksack and following Grandad up two flights of stairs and through a long corridor. He opened the door and there was my mum's room. A long-haired tabby cat lay on the patchwork quilt that covered the bed. She stretched and yawned as we entered.

'That's Martha,' said Grandad, dumping my case on the floor. 'Her grandmother, Penny, was your mother's cat, but she's long gone.' He just stood in the middle of the room with his hands dug deep in his pockets as he stared around him. I unlocked my case and tipped a pile of my clothes on to the floor.

'Well, um, I'll leave you to sort your belongings.' And my grandad backed out like he couldn't wait to leave me.

I sat on the edge of the bed and pulled the tiny piece of paper the rainbow-girl had pressed into my hand out of my jeans pocket.

Before I'd had a chance to take a look, I jumped as the door creaked open. A furry nose peeped through the gap and I breathed a sigh of relief. Lara the retriever padded across the room and put her nose on my lap. I unscrewed the paper. There was a phone number scrawled on it. Underneath it said:

07700 902486
I have been waiting for u.
Seeing as we r going 2 be friends u will need my number –
Megan and Claude, a X and an oink. Text me.

I felt a tiny ray of curious sunshine push through my grey lonely fog. A new friend – that would be more precious to me than all the sparkly treasures on Planet Earth. I gently smoothed out the note and hid it between the pages of my Special Blue Book.

I looked round the room. On the wall next to the bed were pictures of bands I didn't recognize. A glass butterfly mobile caught the light by the window, sending rainbow colours, like the rainbow-girl, shooting through the room. Piles of old teenage magazines lay under the bed, dusty and crumpled, with girls in old-fashioned clothes on the front.

As I opened the door of the old oak wardrobe Martha leaped off the bed and wound herself round my legs. Lara sniffed and pawed at a few old dresses of my mum's that still hung there.

I took a swirly dress of pink silk and buried my face in it, breathing in her scent. I slipped it on over my jeans and T-shirt but my flat chest didn't fill it. I pulled it off and threw it on the bed and picked out a yellow one instead. It fitted perfectly.

I stared at myself in the yellow dress, in the mirror above the oak dressing table. My short scraggy hair stuck up like a circus clown's. I picked up a silver brush that was lying there. It still had one of mum's wavy hairs curled around the bristles. I brushed my stupid hair hard. Martha leaped on to the dressing table, purring.

A breeze brushed against my face and the glass of the butterfly mobile tinkled and spun as an arc of lilac light jumped round the room, dazzling my eyes. Through the sun-droplet haze I could see the shape of my mum as a ten-year-old girl in the yellow dress, smiling and holding her arms out to me. I held out my arms to hug her. Only she wasn't there.

I pulled my new purple phone from my rucksack and texted my mum.

Hug you

I waited and waited but no text came back with 'Hug you more'.

'You'll be wanting something to eat,' said Grandad through the gap in the door. He started in surprise when his eyes fell on me in the yellow dress, his eyes flicking from shock to anger to sadness in less than a blink. Then he swallowed and whispered: 'Why, Grace! It's like seeing your mum standing before me. What's that you've got there?'

'It's my new phone, Grandad. Mum gave it to me.' I held it out to him.

He turned it round in the palm of his huge hairy hand and frowned. 'I don't know, you kids with your newfangled gadgets.'

'I've texted her, Grandad, but she's not texted back.'

'Grace, lass, her phone will be switched off in hospital. It interferes with machinery and hearing aids and all sorts. They're a blessed nuisance. You can write your mum a nice letter.'

'I'd rather text her.'

'We send letters in this house,' said Grandad. 'Now let's be having you. You'll be wanting your tea.'

Pulling off the yellow dress, I followed him

along the corridor and down the stairs, tripping over Lara as I went.

On the table in the gigantic kitchen was an enormous ham, pots of pickle and a massive bowl of potato salad. My tummy was burbling with hunger. It was a long time since the soggy chips. I tucked in.

'Good lass,' said Grandad. 'I can't abide a child with a finicky appetite. Will you be able to occupy yourself this evening by writing to your mum? I've got Mrs Harpson from the village coming up to do my accounts.'

'I'll be fine, Grandad.' I felt a nose on my lap. I sneaked a bit of ham under the table. Lara gobbled it up.

'And there will be no feeding the dog at the table.'

'No, Grandad,' I said, sneaking Lara another bit.

'Right – rules,' said Grandad. 'There has to be rules. You'll mind your Ps and Qs. I can't abide bad manners. And stay away from yon girl with the pig.'

I felt a cross knot pull tight in my tummy.

'But why, Grandad? I'd like to talk to her.'

'You've got this lovely big house to play in. You don't need to be dancing round the farmyard with her, making a menace of yourself. Do you understand? You're a young lady, not a wild animal.' Blah blah blah blah. The knot in my tummy pulled tighter.

'Yes, Grandad. Can I go to my room now?'

'You may leave the table. If you do as I say we'll get along just fine. And keep your room tidy, please. You're to put away those clothes you've tipped on your bedroom floor. I can't abide mess.'

I raced up the stairs to my mum's room, leaped over the pile of clothes, grabbed my purple phone from the bed and started to text.

Hi Megan. This is your new friend Grace. I like your pig Claude. I have never met a pig b4. Will u and Claude show me round the farm please? A x 4 u and a hug and a pat for Claude.

I pressed send . . .

My phone bleeped.

Meet me at the outside bog. Megan x

3

The rainbow-girl was waiting for me. I could see the tip of her red wellie boot peeping round the corner of a small brick shed when I looked out of my bedroom window.

I heaved the bottom part of the sash window up and leaned right out, but she couldn't see me. I gaped at the patchwork quilt of green fields stretching forever, with tiny dotted horses, cows and sheep making patterns as they moved around, pulling at grass. How many million trillion footsteps would it take for me to walk over this green quilt and back to Mum in London?

A car bumped across the farmyard and stopped. I quickly pulled my head back in and slammed the window shut, then peeped back round the curtain. A small lady with short spiky blonde hair, wearing extremely high heels and a brown coat, scrambled out of the car. I guessed she must be Mrs Harpson the accountant, judging by the amount of files she was balancing under her chin as she tottered up to the farmhouse.

I listened at my bedroom door and heard Grandad showing the lady into a room and banging the door. I ran along the corridor and down the stairs, dragging my hand along the wall as I went.

A lady in a flowery overall with her hair in a grey straggly bun stepped out of one of the bedroom doors on the landing in front of me.

'Mind your fingermarks on the banister. It's just been polished.'

I fell down the last two steps of the once-brown threadbare carpet and grabbed the wall.

'You must be Grace. Where are you off to in such a hurry?'

'Just to get a bit of fresh air after my long

journey,' I said, recovering from my surprise and putting on my best ill-face.

'Your grandad's set you up a paper and envelope on the kitchen table for you to write to your mam. He says he'll post it in the morning.' She looked me up and down. 'You do look a bit pasty, lass. A bit of good Yorkshire air'll do you no harm. Don't be long, mind, or your grandad'll have my guts for garters.' Her eyes rested on my trainers.

'You'll be wanting more on your feet than those. Come – I'm Polly, by the way. I come up to the house to do bits and bobs for your grandad.'

I followed Polly down the second staircase and through the kitchen into a dark scullery with a broken light switch. Inside was nothing but an old stone sink and a cupboard.

Polly pulled the cupboard open and out fell a load of wellington boots. She picked out a green pair.

'These used to belong to my daughter, Sarah. Try 'em.'

I pulled off my trainers and hid them right in the corner of the cupboard and heaved my feet into the green wellies. They were a bit big.

'Thanks, Polly,' I said. 'I won't be long.'

'See you're not, mind.' And she disappeared into the kitchen.

I opened the back door and ran towards the small brick shed.

'About time, Grace Wilson,' said the smiling rainbow-girl, stepping out in front of me. 'Thought you'd never come. I'm Megan Haggett and this 'ere pig is Claude.'

Claude was running round and round the brick shed whilst snorting, a red harness trailing behind him.

'I'm very pleased to meet you both,' I stumbled. 'I wasn't sure what a bog was. It was lucky I saw your toe peeping round the wall from my bedroom.'

'Our Grace, don't they teach you anything in them schools in London?' She laughed. 'It's an outside lavvie, look,' and she opened the door and there was an old cracked toilet with a massive spider in the middle of the floor.

Spiders are my worst thing. I backed away.

'It's OK,' said Megan, slamming the door. 'Spiders, they can't hurt ya. Don't let your grandad hear you call it a bog. He'll know you've been knocking about with me. He'll make you call it the outside lavatory. How old are you?'

'Ten years, one month, one week and two days,' I said.

'I'm eleven,' said Megan. 'Come.' She took my hand, grabbed Claude's harness and together we ran, laughing, behind the pig pen, the cowshed and round the barn, with Claude chasing us and pulling us, wrapping his lead round our legs.

We stopped by an old stone wall and pulled ourselves on to it, sitting on its ridge with the stones scraping our legs. I had skinned my elbow. I cuddled the baby pig close.

'Our Claude's taken a fancy to you,' said Megan. She spat and hit the tree by the barn. I tried but could only dribble.

'You'll learn, Our Grace,' she sighed. She

leaned forward to set Claude free and he squealed on the ground. Then she grabbed my hand and pulled me up to stand, wobbling, on the wall with her. We could see over all the hedges and gates, the green patchwork quilt swirling round us. I was as high as the birds. Well, nearly.

'Is this all Grandad's farm?' I gasped.

'Yes, Grace, all that your eyes can see, and more. Our cottage belongs to him and all, so me mam says we have to do as your grandad wishes.'

Then we jumped down, laughing. And we danced as Claude chased us towards the door that once was blue.

The most beautiful lady I had ever seen stepped out of the doorway. She had blonde tangled hair, bright red lips and sparkles in her eyes, and she wore a long flowing black skirt and shawl. She walked slowly towards me and took my chin in her hands. Then she looked deep into my eyes – straight into my soul – and kissed me the sweetest of kisses on my cheek.

'You've come,' she said. 'We've waited so long to see you. I'm Allie, Megan's mam. I know what will warm your heart my pet, after such a long day.' Then she turned to Megan. 'They're ready in the kitchen – you can fetch 'em.'

'Yes, Mam,' said Megan and ran through the door with Claude at her heels.

My heart ached. I thought again of walking the trillion billion steps over the green patchwork quilt to reach my mum in London.

'Wellies off, young lady,' bellowed Allie. A pair of red wellington boots came flying back through the door.

'Come,' said Allie and she put her arm across my shoulder. We walked round the side of the cottage into the back yard, where there was a pen containing two tiny baby lambs.

'They're motherless,' said Allie. 'We're hand-rearing them for your grandad.'

Megan appeared in bright green holey socks with her mucky toes peeping through, holding two bottles of milk. Allie opened the pen and we all knelt on the ground.

'Like this,' said Allie. 'Hold the teat of the bottle or the little beggar will suck it off.'

As the tiny lamb guzzled, happiness tingled up from my toes, reaching my heart and stopping it from aching – just for a moment. Allie sat on the back-door step and, taking out a tin of tobacco and some papers, rolled herself a funny cigarette. As the smoke came out of her nostrils she watched me.

My lamb had finished his bottle just as a lad of about eighteen, tanned brown with cornflower-blue eyes, came round the side of the cottage, swinging a bucket. He was whistling and, as the bucket clanged from side to side, the muscles on his shoulders wriggled.

'This is our Ryan, my big brother,' said Megan without looking up. She gave her lamb its last few drops.

'All right,' said Ryan, nodding to me. 'Mam, have you got any leftover sops to add to the bucket for the pigs?'

'In the yellow bowl in the larder,' said Allie. Ryan put the bucket down behind Megan and went in. There was a bang and a loud squeal and an *oink* as Ryan fell over Claude. Then lots of really rude words – and I mean *really* rude – came flying out of the cottage. I stored them in my head to write in my Special Blue Book to use in my stories and plays.

Allie stood up and went into the cottage, screaming, 'Ryan, wash your mouth out, we've got company!' Then, as Megan stood up, everything seemed to go into slow motion. She stepped backwards, slipped and fell into the pig-swill bucket, showing the world her red knickers. I laughed till I nearly wet myself.

It was that very moment that I knew she was my best friend in the world. I saw a small trickle of blood flow over her hand where she'd caught it on the gravel as she tried to steady herself, and I stepped forward and held out my elbow, where blood still oozed from when I'd skinned it on the wall.

'Sisters,' I said.

She touched my blood to hers.

'Blood sisters till we die,' said Megan.

4

I pulled Megan out of the pig-swill bucket, sops dripping down her legs. Allie was standing in the doorway watching, a smile on her face.

'I need a wee desperate, like one-second-to-spare desperate. Where's your toilet? Please, Allie?' I shouted.

'Go up the stairs and it's right in front of you.' Allie helped me pull my wellies off. 'Run,' she said.

I could hear Claude's tiny feet scampering after me. As I flushed the chain and washed my hands Allie bellowed up the stairs, 'Grace, love, could you fetch our Megan some clean clothes? You'll know her room. It's the one you have to put your shoulder to the door to open, 'cause of all the stuff on the floor.'

I shoved open the door nearest me. Rivers of brightly coloured clothes tumbled out of the wardrobe and drawers, flowing on to the floor and rippling round my feet. I grabbed a pair of jeans and a green jumper and paddled through to pick up a pair of orange knickers dangling from the drawer handle.

As I made my way back out to the landing I heard frightened squealing coming from the room in front of me. I crossed the tiny landing and pushed open the door. There was a huge double bed with a pretty white quilt and deep red curtains and a vase of red roses on a wooden chest. I knelt and looked under the bed. A pair of brown eyes stared out at me. I put out my hands but couldn't reach. The little pig was jammed.

'Don't cry, Claude. I'll get help.' I ran out of the room and down the stairs.

I could hear Allie shouting, 'Hold still, Megan! Do you want me to get the pig swill out of your hair or not?'

'Mam, the water's cold.'

Then murmuring and words came trickling through the hinge. 'Poor pet . . . miserable old . . . hospital . . . *mumble mumble* . . . only family.'

Then a man's voice: 'I know it means the world to you, Allie, seeing her,' followed by more murmuring.

I pushed open the door. Everyone stopped talking about me.

Megan was standing, head over the sink, wrapped in a huge towel, her rainbow clothes in a pile on the floor, with Allie pouring a jug of water over her head. Ryan was sitting at the table eating a cheese sandwich.

'Claude's stuck under your bed, Allie. He's crying.'

A man with a red nose, drinking beer from a bottle, was leaning against the mantelpiece; he walked up to me and ruffled my hair.

'Hello Grace, duck,' and he winked at me. 'I'm Tommy, Megan's dad. I work for your grandad, same as our Ryan.'

'Please come,' I said. 'Claude—'

'Oh, stuck again,' sighed Tommy. 'He'll be the death of me that pig, little beggar.'

Allie was already running up the stairs. I threw the clean clothes to the dripping Megan and ran after Allie, with Tommy huffing and puffing behind me. They both grabbed a corner of the bed.

'One, two, three,' said Allie and they lifted it. I knelt on the floor and reached and grabbed the tiny pig.

'Oh, my back,' said Tommy.

Claude had something in his mouth. I took it gently from him; it was an old dog-eared photograph of my mum, outside the cottage, smiling at the camera – she must have been about twelve, in a grey school uniform. She had a brush in her hand and was painting the front door the brightest of all blues. She had splodges of blue paint on her face and on her school uniform.

I stared at the picture of the girl smiling back at me, a girl with my eyes and smile, but with lovely wavy hair. I touched my own short scraggy hair, hating it.

A young Allie covered in blue paint was sitting on the doorstep in the picture, cigarette in one hand and paintbrush in the other, sticking her tongue out at the camera.

Allie knelt on the floor next to me. 'Thought I'd lost that. Do you know who that is?'

I nodded. 'You knew my mum?'

Allie smiled. 'She were the best friend I ever had till your grandad separated us.' Allie swallowed, her sparkly eyes watering.

'That photo were taken when your mum came to say goodbye, before your grandad sent her away to that posh school. We vowed that the door would not be painted again till we were back together. I miss her.'

'I hate my grandad,' I said.

'You mustn't say that,' said Allie, putting her arm around me. 'Your grandad's not a bad man,' she whispered. 'He's a frightened man. He's scared of joy and laughter. Ever since your granny ran off with her soldier man, your grandad wants everyone around him to walk with their feet firmly on the ground. But your mum, she just loved to dance; she could never keep her feet still. And your grandad thought it were me that were to blame for the wildness in her heart. That it were me that taught her the dancing and how to have joy and laughter, so that's why he stopped us seeing each other and sent her away to that school.'

I kissed the photograph and put it on the wooden chest next to the roses.

There was the sound of feet thundering up the stairs. Megan, dressed in the green jumper and jeans, ran into the room carrying my green wellies.

'That Mrs Harpson, her what does your grandad's numbers, she's driving away in her car. Your grandad'll be looking for you. You've got to get out of here.'

'Run,' said Allie. 'Run home. Don't let your grandad catch you here. Run!'

I slid down the stairs on my bottom, Megan right behind me. She tried to help me but forced my wellies on to the wrong feet. With no time to swap them I ran.

'Bye, Megan,' I yelled, the door that once was blue banging behind me. I raced across the farmyard, through the dusk, past the pig pen, the barn and the cowshed. But as I passed the bog, my wellies flapping, I started to fall, the mud racing towards my face, then up, up, up in the air. I saw cornflower-blue eyes laughing at me as Ryan threw me over the wriggling muscles on his shoulder and ran with me towards the farmhouse.

Pushing the back door slowly open and peering into the dark scullery, he set me on my feet inside the door and crept to the wellington boot cupboard. Feeling inside, he pulled out a small black rubber torch and, switching it on, pressed it into my hand. He put his finger on his lips and vanished.

Holding the torch between my teeth, I pulled off the green wellies and threw them in the cupboard. I shoved my feet back in the trainers that I'd hidden in the corner of the shelf and then ran into the brightly lit kitchen, squeezing the torch into my jeans pocket. There was an envelope, pen and paper set out on the table. I pulled out my Special Blue Book.

I wrote down *bog*. I wrote it over and over: *bog bog bog*.

Then I wrote all the really rude words I'd heard Ryan say, only I can't show you those. Lara padded in and rested her head on my knee, wagging her tail.

I wrote on the piece of paper Grandad had left on the table:

Dear Mum,
Today I met a rainbow-girl

My grandad walked in.

'I've been looking for you high and low. What have you been up to?'

'I've been exploring your house, Grandad,' I said, putting on my best I've-been-here-all-the-time face.

'I've phoned the hospital,' said Grandad.

'Can I talk to Mum please?'

'No, Grace, the nurse said your mum's comfortable – sleeping, she said. You'd best get off to bed. Tomorrow you start school.'

5

Today Grandad is forcing me against my will to start Waldon Primary School. The old goat.

For a second I thought Grandad was going to hug me, but he didn't.

'Mind you behave yourself,' he said. 'No playing silly beggars. I'm off to the market.' And he left me alone at the school gate. The tree above me rustled. A pair of red wellies dangled in front of my nose and out of the branches she dropped, rainbow-girl Megan, standing grinning in front of me.

'I waited till he'd gone,' she said. 'Come.'

My new best friend put her arm round me and pulled me across the school playground, ploughing a path through lanky kids, titchy snotty-nosed kids, scruffy baggy-jumpered boys kicking footballs and chattering nattering girls. The games and gossip slammed to a halt and everyone stared, murmuring into each others' ears.

'What are you all gawping at?' yelled Megan. 'Sisters,' she whispered to me.

'Blood sisters till we die,' I whispered back and touched my elbow to her hand like yesterday, when we became blood sisters.

'I've got to take you to see our Kylie in the school office. She goes out with our Ryan,' she giggled into my ear. 'She's his girlfriend. They kiss, yuck! Who'd kiss our Ryan?' snorted Megan.

The sound of a car horn beeping and loud dance music zinged into my ears. I turned round to see a silver car like celebrities have, with the roof down, pull up outside the school gate. Megan's arm tightened round my shoulders. A girl with long blonde hair and a turned-up nose stepped out; she was carrying a very large pink case a bit like the one Mum used for her make-up, only much bigger.

'That's Lucy Potts,' Megan told me.

A titchy boy with a shaved head, who was cramming lots of Maltesers into his mouth at once, jumped out of the car after her. He scampered to keep up with the girl.

'Lucy, Tom!' shouted a boy with black spiky hair and an earring, breaking from the crowd and running towards them.

'Over here,' shouted a lanky ginger girl who was chasing after him.

But Lucy pushed past them and walked straight towards me, smiling. Megan wasn't smiling.

'You must be the new girl. You're going to be in my class – Year Five, Miss Sams. You're going to sit next to me. We've cleared a space.'

'Thanks, Lucy.' I smiled at her.

Megan scuffed her wellington toe in the dirt.

'It's Talk About Your Hobby Assembly, and it's my turn this week. You can have a look if you want.' She put the pink case on the ground and started fiddling with the clasp.

'We've got to go, Grace,' said Megan, tugging at my arm.

The case fell open. Inside was a miniature hairdressing salon with polystyrene heads with wigs of every shade, weaved and plaited into different styles.

There were sprays and potions and brushes, combs and clips and ribbons of every colour of the rainbow, and mini hairdryers. It was the most amazing thing I have ever seen in my ten years and one month and a week and three days of being on Planet Earth. I put out my hands to stroke a red spiky wig.

'Dad bought it for me. He's going to buy me my own salon when I'm eighteen. This is just to practise on,' said Lucy. 'It's taken me hours to get all these wigs styled for today.'

'I helped,' said the girl with ginger hair.

'You helped a *bit*, Hannah,' said Lucy.

She picked up one of the plastic heads with a wig on it; a French plait that was coming unravelled.

'Oh, look what's happened, Hannah. You're rubbish at hair.'

'I . . .' stumbled Hannah, burning red.

'Don't worry,' I said. 'I'll fix it.' I sat cross-legged on the ground and quickly started weaving my fingers in and out, re-doing the French plait.

'Grace, come on,' said Megan.

'You're good at styling,' said Lucy. 'You can come round to my house and I'll let you do some work in my mini salon if you want.'

'Thanks, Lucy,' I said, feeling sunny inside.

Megan spat and it hit the school wall.

Lucy crinkled up her nose.

'You can hang out with us – can't she, Robert?' she said to the boy with the black hair and earring.

'Uh-huh,' agreed the boy.

'Tom,' Lucy turned to the titchy boy with the shaved head, 'since my dad gave you a lift, you could at least share those Maltesers with us and stop scoffing them all at once.'

Lucy snatched the packet and poured some

into my hand. Megan grabbed my arm and started to pull me up from the floor. Some of the Maltesers went bouncing across the yard.

'We've got to go and see our Kylie. Come on, Grace.'

I pulled my arm away. 'In a minute, Megan, I've not quite finished.'

Smack! A football hit Megan on the side of her head. Her eyes watered for a second and I held my breath, but then she grabbed the ball and kicked it hard, scoring a goal. A crowd of the scruffy baggy-jumpered boys surrounded her, cheering, and dragged her off to join in their game.

I grabbed a band and fastened it to the end of the plait. Straightening the wig on the polystyrene head, I brushed the fringe. Then I picked up a purple silky ribbon and let it run through my fingers.

Lucy whispered, tickling in my ear, 'You can come to tea tonight – we are having a barbecue and I've got a new make-up set with twelve different nail varnishes. I'll let you try them all.'

'Thanks, Lucy,' I said, the sunbeams inside getting warmer. 'I'll ask Grandad.' I weaved the purple ribbon through the French plait.

'That looks lovely,' said Lucy. 'You're brilliant at hair. I will definitely give you a job when you are grown up – in the salon my dad's going to buy me.'

'Thank you,' I said, the sun scorching me.

'You could style Megan's hair,' said Lucy.

'Oh, I'd love to,' I laughed. 'Her hair's wild.'

'It's all tangled and messy,' sniggered Lucy. 'She's in Year Six and she can't even brush her hair.'

The sun disappeared behind a cloud. 'She can,' I said. 'She just doesn't want to. Her hair's so gorgeous.'

'You don't want to hang around with smelly cowpat-girl Megan, no one likes her,' said Lucy.

'*I* do,' I said.

'But she wears those minging red wellies all the time. Do you like my new trainers? Look, they're the same pink as my hairdressing-salon case. Come on, *I'll* take you to the school office,' said Lucy, putting her arm around me.

The sun inside me turned to rain as dark clouds danced behind my eyes.

'Megan is my best friend,' I said, pushing her arm away hard. 'I think her curly hair is beautiful. And no, I don't like your pink trainers; I love Megan's red wellies. I wish I had a pair.'

I dumped the newly styled wig in the case and stood up. Lucy's jaw dropped open like a crazy goldfish. She snapped her pink case shut and stormed off. Hannah and Tom ran after her.

'Oy, what have you said to her, London-girl?' said Robert as he poked me hard in the ribs.

'Oh, bog off, Robert,' yelled Megan, racing across the playground towards me. Grabbing my arm, she pulled me away from him, towards a door that stood open.

'Oy, Grace.'

I turned round. Tom, Hannah and Robert were all in a huddle around sulky Lucy.

'You'll be sorry,' screeched Lucy.

'Sorry for what?' asked Megan as Lucy's screech rang in my ears.

'Oh, Lucy invited me to tea to play with her stupid hairdressing salon and I didn't want to,' I lied. Well, it was only half a lie really so I hoped it didn't count. 'Cause all I did was leave stuff out – all the spiteful disgusting things she'd said about Megan.

I followed her through the door into an office. A very pretty lady with long black hair and laughing green eyes was sorting out a pile of exercise and reading books.

'Kylie, this is our Grace,' said Megan, pushing me in front of her.

The lady gave me a kind smile and squeezed

my arm. 'Megan, how many times? It's Miss Princeton at school.'

Megan rolled her eyes to the ceiling. 'Me brother said to tell you, our Claude's gone and run off with his phone in his mouth and hidden it again, so he can't phone you about the pictures tonight. He says he'll pick you up about seven – and can I come, Miss Princeton?'

'No, Megan, you can't,' laughed Kylie.

Pointing to a five-a-day fruit and vegetable poster and putting her finger over her lips, she opened the top drawer of her desk and took out two Mars bars.

'I won't tell if you don't,' she said, winking. 'Off you go to Assembly, Megan,' she said, throwing one of the Mars bars to her.

She pressed the other one into my hand. 'For later – a little something for your break.'

'Thanks, Miss Princeton,' I said. Megan started unwrapping hers.

'Megan, Assembly, now! Grace'll be fine with me. Go.'

Megan pulled a face. 'See you later, Grace,'

she said, jumping up and swinging from the top of the doorframe. Then she was gone.

'There you go, all your books for Year Five,' said Kylie as she handed me the pile from her desk.

'Thank you, miss,' I said, dropping half of them as I scrabbled to stuff all the new books in my purple rucksack, but they wouldn't fit. I put the Mars bar safely away in the front pocket.

'Um, Grace, have they let you speak to your mum yet after the operation?'

I pretended to reshuffle the books in my bag as I shook my head. Kylie knelt down on the floor next to me, took the books out, repacked them and fastened my rucksack.

'Grace, any time you want a chat you just come and find me.'

'My mum will be dancing round the house when I call her, miss. She probably won't hear the phone 'cause her music's up too loud.'

'That she will, Grace, she'll be fine,' she said. 'Come on, I'll take you down to Assembly.'

Kylie tottered next to me in her high heels,

clickerty clack, down a long, long corridor, her mouth going *chat chat chat*. I was saying, 'Yes,' in my best polite voice in all the right places, but inside I felt sick to my toes. There was a sign on the wall that said:

If you are lucky enough to have a phone, switch it off or leave it at home!

I felt for my phone in my pocket and switched it to silent. In my head I was chanting: *Text me, Mum. Text me please*, over and over – willing Mum to send me a 'Hug you more' text to tell me they were letting her out of the hospital.

There was no way on Planet Earth I was ever switching my phone off or leaving it at home.

Kylie put her finger to her lips as we reached a door at the end of the corridor.

'Shhhh, Mr Grantham's started Assembly.' She opened the door a crack and beckoned to someone.

A lady with dangly earrings and long red hair came to the door.

'Hello. Grace, I'm Miss Sams. Let's see if we can find you a seat,' she whispered.

We crept in. On the stage was the headmaster. Mr Grantham was an old man, though not as old as Grandad, and was bald with a big belly and glasses. He looked kind. Next to him sat Lucy Potts with her pink case, like a queen on her throne.

There was an empty chair in the back row. Megan grinned and waved to me from her place at the front. I tripped and bumped over knees and feet, trying to be invisible and get to the seat. As I climbed over Robert's feet he kicked me in the shin.

'Ah! Our new girl has joined us,' came a booming voice from the stage. I froze.

'This is Grace.' My legs turned to jelly. 'Grace is from London and I hope you'll all make her welcome at Waldon Primary School,' said Mr Grantham. Everyone stared and started whispering.

'Shhhh now. I taught Grace's mother, Chloe, a long time ago – when I still had hair,' said Mr

Grantham, tapping his bald head.

A crackling of laughter.

'Grace, it's so lovely to have you here and I do hope that you'll be very happy with us.'

I stumbled over the last few pairs of feet and at last reached my seat. I sat.

'Grace.'

I stood back up again.

'Today is our special Hobby Assembly – may I ask if you have any hobbies?'

I had a tonsil jam, then I heard myself squeak. 'Clarinet and tap dancing, sir.' I collapsed, burning red, on to the chair.

'Splendid, splendid!' said Mr Grantham. 'Now, if you would all shut your eyes in prayer.'

A shuffling of feet and coughing.

'Our Father in heaven, please look over and protect all the ex-pupils of Waldon Primary School. Especially those who have moved away from Yorkshire.'

He was praying for my mum. I shivered.

'Protect the sick and their loved ones.'

I double-dared myself to look up. Megan had

her eyes screwed up tight and brushed something from her cheek. It can't have been a teardrop, it must have been the light.

I looked up through the hall roof to heaven and chanted over and over again in my head: *Mum got her lump dancing. Mum got her lump dancing.*

Mr Grantham was staring straight at me. I quickly shut my eyes and looked down.

The prayer murmured to an end.

Lucy strutted to the middle of the stage with her pink case and opened it and droned on and on – *blah blah blah* – about how she had personally styled all the wigs. Mr Grantham did a tiny secret yawn and took a peep at his watch. He thought no one saw but I did.

Then Lucy told a juicy fat lie. She held out the wig I had styled and said, 'I am especially good at French plaits. This is one I did earlier.' She stared at me. I stared back. Our eyes glued with *hate*.

My phone vibrated in my pocket. I eased it out slowly, slowly, so as not to be seen.

You have 1 message. I touched the screen. **Hug you more, my darling. They r—**

'Mr Grantham, Mr Grantham,' screeched Lucy. 'Our new girl is distracting me. She's using her phone. How can I talk about my mini hairdressing salon when our new girl is reading a text?'

Mr Grantham stood up. 'Grace, as it's your first day I will let you off, but what is our rule, everyone?'

'*If you are lucky enough to have a phone, switch it off or leave it at home*,' droned the whole school but me.

And then I couldn't help it. I know my eyes should have been giving my best sorry-sir look to Mr Grantham but they flicked back down to the text instead. I had to read Mum's message.

They r keeping me—

'PASS ME THE PHONE,' boomed Mr Grantham. 'How dare you look at your text when I am talking to you?'

Two hundred eyes stung me as Mr Grantham marched off the stage and down the side of the hall. His kindness had turned to ice.

I pressed menu on the touch screen to hide my text before the girl next to me snatched my phone. And Mum's message that I hadn't even had a chance to read, disappeared as hand after hand snatched and grabbed and passed Mum's text further and further away from me.

When my phone reached Robert, I saw him quickly press the touch screen on my phone a few times and then mutter something.

'ROBERT!' shouted Mr Grantham.

'I am just turning it off for you, sir.'

My purple phone reached Mr Grantham and he put Mum's message in his pocket.

'Young lady, it's very rude to look at your phone when Lucy is kindly telling us about her most interesting hobby. Collect it from my office at the end of the day.'

I stood up and heard myself say, 'Please, sir – *please* can I have my phone back?'

There was a gasp and then whispering,

which grew and grew into a swarm of angry bees.

'Please, sir, our Grace needs her phone,' said Megan, suddenly standing up at the front of the hall. 'It's her ma—'

'QUIET!' boomed Mr Grantham. 'Megan Haggett, where there's trouble why are you always in the middle of it? Grace, I don't know how you were allowed to behave at your school in London but in Waldon Primary we do not answer back. Do you understand?'

'But, sir, I need—'

'Do you understand?'

'Yes, sir, but—'

'QUIET! This is not a good beginning, is it? Back to your classes, everyone.'

And he marched out of the hall with my world in his pocket.

Megan pulled a face as her class were led past me.

'See you at break,' she mouthed.

I was swept along, squashed in the middle of Miss Sams' class.

Tramping stamping feet all around me – along a corridor with Year One paintings on the wall. I noticed one with a stick-lady smiling and holding a stick-child's hand with 'Mummy and me' painted in red, the drawing pins coming loose. Next to it was a door to the playground.

We came to a stop at a classroom door, right at the end of the corridor. Chatter, laughter and screaming zinged in my ears as everyone found their seat but I had nowhere to go. I stood at the front of the class, feeling sick to my toes. A hushed silence fell over the room, everyone's eyes on me, waiting.

Lucy's eyes threw knives of hate. There was an empty desk next to her.

'I have put you next to Lucy. She'll look after you.'

'Please, Miss Sams, I can look after myself. I don't need to sit next to Lucy,' I said.

The swarm of angry bees started whispering again.

'QUIET!' yelled Miss Sams, reddening. 'Grace, we want to welcome you as part of our class. So please come and sit with Lucy and be part of the group.'

Then Miss Sams wrote some rubbish sums on the whiteboard but I couldn't concentrate. The numbers danced and spun.

Lucy Potts smirked. 'I've still got *my* lovely pink glittery phone, Grace. You need to watch yourself, you do.' Then she turned back to the board with dancing numbers on it.

* * *

Through the morning the numbers gave way to the swirling rivers of Geography, which flowed into the crumbling castles of History – but all I could think of was Mum's text.

I ached from head to toe to be back at 22 Manderly Road, Southgate, North London, and look after Mum, so she would get better and we could dance around the house again with the music turned up really loud.

At break Megan waited for me in the yard.

'Oh our Grace, on your first day as well. Even I didn't get into that much trouble.'

She pulled funny faces to try and cheer me up. It didn't work, so we ate our Mars bars sitting on the bottom rung of a climbing frame.

At dinner she queued up with me, got me a tray and helped me choose the food for my plate. Shepherd's pie and chips. But as I chewed, all I could think of was my purple phone with Mum's text sitting in the headmaster's office.

The minutes of the afternoon crawled along. It felt like years had gone by when the bell rang for the end of the day.

Megan was waiting outside my classroom. We ran to Mr Grantham's office and knocked on the door.

'COME IN!' he yelled.

'We've come for our Grace's phone, sir.'

'Ah, yes.' He reached in his top drawer. 'I'm going to stand here and watch you and make sure you don't switch it on again till you are out of the school gates. Do you understand?'

'Thank you, sir. Sorry, sir,' I said.

'Oh and Grace, how's your mum?'

'She don't know, sir,' said Megan. 'That's why she needed her phone – to find out.'

'Oh,' said Mr Grantham, his chin hitting his collar.

He opened a door that led directly on to the yard. We walked through, then ran and ran to the school gates. I could feel Mr Grantham's eyes drilling holes in the back of my shoulder blades. But I could feel another pair of eyes on me too. I turned my head and there was Lucy Potts, throwing darts of hate at me from the top bar of the climbing frame.

Polly was waiting at the school gate to walk me home. As soon as we were outside the gate, with shaking hands, I switched on my phone and went to texts.

Hug you more, my darling. They r keeping me in hospital a little longer. Nothing 2 worry about. Operation went v well. B good. Luv u so much,

Mum xxxxx

'Polly, please, I need to speak to Mum. I need to phone the hospital. I don't have the number. I don't have enough credit.'

'Don't fret lass, we'll phone her from your grandad's phone before he gets back from market,' said Polly, putting her hand on my shoulder.

My phone bleeped. **You have 1 message.** I touched the screen.

Ur mum dumped u here coz she does not want to c ur ugly face or ur short ugly hair. If u show this txt to smelly cowpat-girl u r dead.

I turned back to the climbing frame. Robert,

Tom and Hannah had joined Lucy swinging from the top bar and were staring straight at me, stinging me with their eyes.

Robert must have got my number from my phone when it had been passed down the line to Mr Grantham.

'What's up, Grace?' said Megan, following my eyes. 'Have they been bothering you again?'

I looked my best friend straight in the eye and I felt sick to my toes as I told her a big fat lie.

'No, everything's fine,' I said, and switched off my phone.

Polly looked from me to Megan then back to me again.

'Oh, I wondered how long it'd be before you two were as thick as thieves.'

I held my breath. Then she grinned. 'It's all right – don't look so worried, I won't tell your grandad. Come on, quick sharp, let's go and phone your mam.'

'Run, Megan,' I shouted, and we tore down the country lanes all the way back to the farm, Polly huffing and puffing behind us.

'Bye, Megan, best friends forever,' I yelled after her as she disappeared through the door that once was blue.

She turned and yelled back, 'Blood

sisters till we die.'

I sprinted across the farmyard to the back door, through the scullery and into the big kitchen, throwing my purple rucksack in the corner. I waited by the phone, jumping up and down, itching for Polly to catch up.

'Let me get my breath.' Polly staggered through the door.

'Please, please, Polly, I want to phone now, before Grandad gets home and makes me write a letter instead.'

I hopped on one foot as Polly slowly, slowly rummaged through Grandad's cracked old leather address book till she at last found H. She dialled and asked to be put through to Darwin Ward. After what seemed like forever and ever, Polly said in a posh phone voice, 'Hello, I have Chloe Wilson's daughter here. Is it convenient for her to speak to her mother? . . . Oh, thank you.'

I snatched the phone. After a while the phone line clicked and I heard Mum's voice.

'Hello, Grace, my darling.'

I forced the sob jammed in my tonsils back down.

I put on my best I-am-not-going-to-show-you–I-am-frightened face, even though Mum couldn't see it as she was many million trillion footsteps away on the other end of the phone in London.

'Grace? Grace, is it you?'

'Yes, Mum, it's me.' I swallowed. 'Has the lump gone? Why won't they let you out of hospital?'

'Yes, darling, it's gone. But I've got a bit of an infection. Just a little one, silly me,' she said. 'They want it to go before they let me come home. How was your first day at school?'

'I've got a new best friend – her name's Megan and she has a pig called Claude.'

'Oh, how lovely. A little piggy!'

Mum sounded weird. Her voice was over-bright and shiny and she was talking to me like I was three or something, not ten years and five weeks and three days.

'And when they let me out, Mrs Johnson is

going to look after me – isn't that nice?' she said.

Tiny hailstones of anger fizzled in my tummy.

'No, Mum, it's not nice. I'll look after you.'

'Grace, you can't look after me, darling. You have to go to school.'

'I'll leave school. Rubbish sums are a waste of time anyway. I'll become your nurse. I'd be a good nurse. I'll brush your hair every day and we'll dance around the house when you are feeling better with the music turned up really, really loud and we'll eat chocolate.'

'No, Grace.'

'I'll let you have all the strawberry creams. Chocolate always makes you feel better.'

'No, Grace, darling, I need lots of sleep.'

'I'll let you sleep. I'll be as quiet as a tiny mouse.'

'Grace, if you want to help me feel better, you've got to promise me you'll stay in Yorkshire with Grandad and go to school. Go on, promise me.'

'I promise,' I said, but my fingers were crossed.

'Grace, I want you to have lots of fun with your new best friend Megan and her little piggy.'

Then she did that laugh again, the one that didn't tinkle but sounded like a donkey with tummy ache. And it wasn't the tiniest bit funny that she wouldn't let me come home and eat chocolate and dance around the house with her and brush her hair.

There was a silence that threatened to swallow me up forever.

'Grace, I love you so much.'

I knew that I should say something nice and kind and good but the hailstones started to sting, and I just felt so angry at the lump, and at Mum for getting the lump – even though that didn't make any sense 'cause you should be kind to sick people, not angry. And then the words came out and cut my tongue.

'Why should I do what you tell me? Telling me to keep your stupid promise? You don't keep your promises. I've met her, Mum. I've met Allie and you've not painted her front door blue. It's chipped and shabby and it's waiting for you to paint it, Mum, and you haven't. You said you would but you lied.'

All I could hear were sobs.

'Mum, Mum, I'm sorry – I didn't mean to make you cry.' I felt sick to my toes.

'I'm crying because I'm happy, Grace. I didn't know Allie still lived in the cottage. I assumed she'd moved on. We lost touch. Our lives parted. She was my best friend.'

I should've said 'Hug you'. I wish I had but I didn't. The hailstones fizzled up again and more words just tumbled out, slicing me deeper. 'Well, guess what, Mum? Megan is Allie's daughter and I will never ever break a promise to her. Allie, Megan and Claude all live in the cottage and it's got the most shabby chipped door you ever saw just 'cause you haven't painted it. And Grandad won't let Megan and me be friends but I won't let him part us. Not like you did. You let him send you away to that school to stop you being friends with Allie.'

I knew I was being cruel and nasty with a

storm raging around my body, but I felt cut to bits.

'Hug you,' said Mum.

But I couldn't say 'Hug you more' back. I opened my mouth but my tonsils jammed again. I slammed the phone down and ran out of the kitchen.

I didn't stop running till I reached my bedroom and kicked the door shut. I threw myself on the bed, nearly landing on Martha, who yowled and then nuzzled up to me, purring.

Then I did what I always do when I have a storm inside me. I reached for my Special Blue Book. But with a stab in my belly button I realized that my rucksack was downstairs.

I lay on my tummy for what seemed like forever and ever, pushing scary thoughts of lumps and infections and nasty texts out of my brain. I counted the days till the Easter holidays: four weeks and four days.

I heard Grandad come in with Lara, who was barking. I heard a crash as something smashed, then Grandad shouting, 'Lara, you bad, bad dog.'

There was a knock at the door. I sat up and hugged my knees to my tummy and ignored it. The door opened anyway. It was Polly with my purple rucksack and a tray with a chicken and coleslaw sandwich, a packet of cheese-and-onion crisps and a can of Sprite.

'Lara's knocked the stew off the table and gobbled it all up. Your grandad's seeing red, he were that hungry. Thought you might need your bag and a little something to tide you over before I fix summat else for your dinner.' She put the tray on the bed in front of me and stood there looking down at me.

'Anyroad, I've told him you're stopping up here to do your homework – I thought it best. He's not right good at feelings, your grandad.' Then she kissed me on the top of my head and walked out of the door. I scrabbled through my bag and found my Special Blue Book. I started to write as the scary thoughts came trickling back into my brain.

I AM SHUTTING MY EYES TIGHT but peeping through my eyelashes to write this and filling my head with HAPPY THOUGHTS OF CLAUDE AND MEGAN AND DAFT DOG LARA KNOCKING EVERYONE OVER AND GOBBLING UP THE STEW.

I do not want to think about the bad words I said to Mum on the phone. I DO NOT WANT to see in my head THE SCARY WORDS THAT came up on the COMPUTER SCREEN WHEN I GOOGLED LUMP. The words are jumping behind my eyes. I am thinking of how Grandad's face must have looked when Lara ate his stew. It did say on the computer that a lump can just be caused by an injury. It did say that.

Mum must have got her lump when she knocked herself dancing.

MUM GOT HER LUMP DANCING

MUM GOT HER LUMP DANCING

MUM GOT HER LUMP DANCING.

MUM GOT—

A cold breeze brushed my cheek as the glass butterflies on the mobile tinkled and spun faster and faster, sending rainbow lights shooting into my eyes. I wanted so much to see my mum sitting there, holding her arms out to me. I waited and waited but she didn't come.

9

I jolted awake. My phone was bleeping and for one happy second I thought I was at home in London snuggled under my purple quilt. Then – *bang* – the sorry disaster phone call with Mum kicked me in the tummy as the darkness of the room choked me. A light shone from my phone as it bleeped again. I reached out to grab it, my hand accidentally knocking Martha who must have been asleep on the corner of the bed. She hissed and a pair of green eyes lit up the darkness for a second, then vanished as she jumped off the bed. The time on my phone said it was three o'clock in the morning.

You have 1 message.

I was praying over and over again: *Please let it be a 'Hug you' from Mum. Please,* please *let it be.*

I touched the screen.

Go back 2 London where u belong. U r ugly. We do not want u at school. Leave now. U show this txt 2 minging Megan & u will be sorry.

I dropped my phone. This sound filled the room like an animal caught in a trap. Only it wasn't an animal, it was coming from inside me, filling my body and stabbing my bones. I curled into a ball and rocked until my anger fled into the dark night and the sadness came. I wanted to hug my mum, tell her I was sorry. A wet nose pushed into my hand and it was Lara, and she was licking the tears on my cheek that I didn't even know were there. She scrambled on to the bed and pushed her way into the curled-up ball of my body till my head was on her head, and I wrapped my arms around her and we rocked together slowly, slowly.

* * *

Someone was shaking my shoulder. I opened one eye: it was Grandad.

'Wakey, wakey – rise and shine. Breakfast's on table. Don't dawdle – you mustn't be late for school.'

A picture of Lucy Potts dressed head to toe in pink sequins, standing in front of a glittery pink door with a flashing sign saying *Lucy's Hair Salon* flashed into my still-dreaming brain. I remembered the night-time text that I felt sure was from Lucy and I felt sick to my toes. I did not want to go to Waldon School ever again as long as I lived on Planet Earth.

The quilt moved. Lara's head peeped over the top.

'Get down those stairs, you daft dog. Go on – basket, now!' said Grandad.

Lara whined, licked me on the nose and was gone.

'Dog's meant to sleep downstairs and she knows it,' said Grandad but he didn't sound too cross.

'Grandad, I think I might have a contagious disease. It would be wrong to go to school and spread my germs. It's best if I stay at home with you. I could help with the cows.' I did my best I-have-a-contagious-disease face.

'Rubbish! Up you get,' said Grandad.

Polly stuck her head round the door.

'She does look a bit pasty,' she said. 'Maybe she's coming down with something?'

'Nothing that a good breakfast and a brisk walk to school won't cure,' said Grandad.

After breakfast, the old goat marched me down the lanes to school.

'Mind you behave yourself,' he growled and then he was gone.

From the tree dangled a pair of red wellie boots and down she dropped, my best friend on Planet Earth.

'I thought you were never going to come. Are you all right, our Grace?'

And I looked my best friend in the eye and lied again.

'Yes,' I said, 'I'm OK,' and I touched my elbow to her hand.

'Come,' she said. 'Teach me how to tap dance,' and she dragged me behind the girls' toilets.

I taught Megan how to do a time step and a shuffle hop step ball change, and it was so funny watching her trying to tap dance in her red wellies, that just for a moment I forgot my phone call with Mum and the night-time texts. Then my phone bleeped and there it was:

Hug you xx

I texted straight back:

Hug u more xxx

Sunshine and laughter rushed into my tummy then ran away again as the school bell rang. I walked slowly, slowly into the class- room. Lucy Potts was sitting in her place, waiting. My empty desk was next to hers.

'I'm going to get you, Grace Wilson,' she mouthed.

All day it was: 'Miss Sams, the new girl jogged me.'

I said nothing.

'Miss Sams, the new girl keeps fidgeting.'

I said nothing.

'Miss Sams, Miss Sams, the new girl isn't doing her maths, she is writing in a little blue book under the table.'

'MY NAME IS GRACE!' I screamed as something deep down inside me smashed to smithereens. 'Get it right, Lucy. It is not "new girl".'

'Get outside. Stand in the corridor till you have cooled off,' said Miss Sams.

'But I—'

'Now, Grace, please,' said Miss Sams, red in the face.

Lucy smirked. The rest of the class stared at me with stupid gaping mouths, all except a small girl with mousy plaits who gave me a little smile. I quickly hid my Special Blue Book under my jumper as I tried to reach into my bag for my phone.

'LEAVE YOUR BAG AND GET INTO THE CORRIDOR NOW!' shouted Miss Sams.

I stormed out of the room. The corridor was cold and lonely. I could hear a squeaking coming from the next classroom. There was a sign on the door that said:

Mrs Patterson – Year Four

I peeped through the door. The noise was coming from a hamster in his cage, running round and round on its squeaking wheel. The room was empty. I could see Year Four through the far window doing P.E. in the playground.

I opened the door and crept in. There was a notice above the cage that said:

My name is Ivan. Please handle me gently.

I opened the cage door and carefully picked up

the little golden creature. I held him on my shoulder; he nuzzled into my ear and tickled me.

The door slammed behind me. It was Lucy Potts.

'Put Ivan back in his cage now before he bites you, London-girl. You were meant to be standing in the corridor, not playing with Year Four's hamster. It's a good thing I caught you. I have been sent with a note for the headmaster. Miss Sams trusts me to run errands.'

I put Ivan back into his cage, then ran back into the corridor.

Lucy pushed past me and went to Ivan's cage. As she came back into the corridor she closed the classroom door behind her and sneered, 'I just had to make sure you closed the cage properly, London-girl.'

When the bell rang for break I went back into my classroom to get my bag. I reached in for my phone but it had gone.

'Miss Sams – please, please I have to find my phone. My mum—'

Lightning bolts of panic shot through me. A search of the school was ordered. Megan was sent for and put her arm around me as we retraced all my steps. We searched round the back of the girls' toilets where I had taught her tap dancing – but it wasn't there.

'Megan, I know it was in my bag,' I said. 'It's been stolen.' I could see the caretaker going through all the bins.

'We'll find it, Grace,' she said, giving me a kiss on the cheek. 'Now where else have you been? Think.'

I took her hand and we entered Year Four's classroom. I walked over to Ivan's cage. There, peeping through the sawdust, was something purple. Megan opened the cage and picked up Ivan. I reached in and buried my hand in the sawdust and pulled out my phone.

As the lightning bolts of panic turned to calm, a wave of sorrow rippled through me. My new purple phone was no longer shiny. It was scratched, with little teeth marks on it.

'Grace, you must've dropped it when you

picked up our Ivan,' said Megan, trying to shine my phone on her violet stripy jumper.

'Yes I must have,' I lied, even though I knew with every bone in my body that I hadn't. Lucy must have stolen it and dropped it in Ivan's cage when she pretended to check I had closed it properly.

I wanted so badly to tell Megan the truth but the text threats jammed my tonsils.

I switched on my phone to check it was working. I touched the screen and opened up texts. The two bullying texts had been deleted.

'What's wrong, our Grace? Something's up,' said Megan.

'I'm OK, Megan, honest,' I lied again. I made a vow that from now on the only thing on Planet Earth I could tell my frightening secret to was my Special Blue Book.

I, Grace Wilson of 22 Manderly Road, Southgate, North London, vow in my heart to only tell my secrets to my Special Blue Book.

Reason 1

I OBVIOUSLY don't want to die if I show the texts to Megan. It would make Mum very sad.

Reason 2

I don't want my best friend Megan to know that Lucy's gang call her smelly cowpat-girl and other things behind her back.

Reason 3

I don't want Megan to think I am a Year Five baby and can't stand up for myself — after all I am only 10 and 5 weeks and 4 days, and Megan is 11 and in Year 6.

I cannot tell Mum as I DON'T WANT TO MAKE HER LUMP HURT. I cannot tell Grandad. He just wouldn't understand.

Every night when I am asleep my phone bleeps and I get another text I copy them down here. These were all in one week.

<u>Monday</u>

U stink of cowpat LIKE UR FRIEND farm-girl.

<u>Tuesday</u>

U look like a boy with ur short ugly hair.

<u>Wednesday</u>

Go back to London where u belong.

<u>Thursday</u>

We don't want u in our SCHOOL. U & MEGAN R MINGERS with ur ugly hair. Go back 2 London & take Megan & her minging red wellies with u.

<u>Friday</u>

Y R U STILL HERE????

They are still sitting in my inbox.

The days did tiny slow footsteps along the path of time but now they are running. There is only one week and four days left till the Easter holidays.

EVERY MORNING Grandad marches me across the farmyard and we see Allie sitting on the doorstep of the door that once was blue, smoking one of her funny cigarettes. She watches me. Grandad and Allie do a tiny little nod to each other, then turn away.

Every day Grandad leaves me at the school gate, looks like he is almost going to hug me but doesn't, then off he goes. The trees rustle and a pair of red wellies dangle in front of my nose and down drops my rainbow-girl Megan. We link arms and run laughing, twirling, spinning, tap dancing through the school playground – my best friend and me. And I forget about the night-time texts just for a moment till I see Lucy Potts and her gang – Robert, Hannah and Tom – standing at the school gate stinging me with their eyes, though I've done nothing to hurt them. They bump me, hold their legs out to trip me when Megan is not looking, and take things off my dinner plate when I look the other way.

Every day Lucy Potts tells tales to Miss Sams about me. Every day I am sent to stand in the corridor. I like it best when Year 4 are doing P.E. so that I can sneak in to see Ivan. We have become good friends.

Every day Lucy Potts mouths at me, 'I AM GOING TO GET YOU, GRACE WILSON.'

THE LAST DAY OF SCHOOL BEFORE THE HOLIDAYS HAS ARRIVED.

10

They have let Mum out of hospital. Polly bought me a top-up for my phone with the ten pounds my dad gave me before he left, so I can phone Mum at home. But only quick calls so I don't run out of credit.

Mum's voice is still over-bright and shiny but I try to keep warm sunshine in my voice as I whisper to her down the phone in case Grandad is listening. I've told Mum about Megan and me playing, dancing and laughing in wellies by the outside bog, behind the pig pen, the cowshed and round the barn, with Claude chasing us and pulling us, wrapping his lead round our legs.

Yesterday Mum laughed her proper silvery tickly laugh, not the one that sounds like a donkey with tummy ache.

Today I phoned before school, but Mrs Johnson answered instead of Mum.

'Grace, love, your mum can't come to the phone today.'

'Why not?' I said.

'She has been back to the hospital for a check-up and now she is feeling very tired. She's been sick a few times. She'll talk to you tomorrow. Goodbye, Grace.'

'Mrs Johnson, Mrs Johnson, wait,' I said before she put the phone down. 'She's been dancing too much, hasn't she, Mrs Johnson?' I said.

Mrs Johnson sounded a bit puzzled. 'No, dear, she's been resting.'

I expect Mum dances when Mrs Johnson isn't around 'cause Mrs Johnson is too old to dance.

'Get a move on, Grace, I've cows want seeing to before I go t'market,' roared Grandad up the stairs.

I quickly said bye to Mrs Johnson, grabbed

my purple rucksack and slid down the stairs on my bottom.

I could hear all the Haggetts shouting at each other from behind the door that once was blue as Grandad walked me across the farmyard on the way to school. I could hear Megan's voice shouting loudest, 'Our Claude was only playing.'

Grandad muttered, 'Oh, they're a noisy lot, Grace. You make sure you stay away.'

'Yes, Grandad,' I said, but I had my fingers crossed.

'And I wish they would give that door a lick of paint. It's a disgrace.'

'They can't, Grandad,' I said.

'What do you mean, lass? Don't talk rubbish. Of course they can.'

I froze, cussing myself for the slip of my tongue.

Tommy saved me, bursting through the door that once was blue and tottering up to me and ruffling my hair.

'All right Grace, duck,' he said with a wink, then toppled off to work in the fields.

I walked slowly, slowly, so that Megan would have a chance to leave the cottage, take the short cut and be there before me, waiting in her tree.

'Stop dawdling, Grace,' said Grandad. 'What's got into you? I've got work to do and market to get to. Get a move on.'

'I'm sorry, Grandad,' I said, doing my best I-am-trying-to-walk-quickly face but still walking as slowly as I could. When we reached the school gate Grandad, the same as every day, looked like he was going to hug me, then didn't, said goodbye and went off to the market. I waited under the tree. I waited and waited and waited, but no Megan dropped from its branches. Where was Megan? I decided to hide in the girls' toilet till the bell rang for Assembly.

I stood in the end cubicle and ran my fingers over the ancient ridges where people had carved their names on the wall. Dan, Garry, Emily, Sally, then right in the middle I saw it. Chloe. I laid my cheek against my mother's graffiti and shut my eyes.

I shivered as a cold breeze surrounded me, making my hair stand on end. I heard laughing in the next cubicle, then a 'Shhh' and a choked giggle. A mist of cigarette smoke floated under the partition. I knelt on the floor to look under it to sneak a peek at who was there. My eleven-year-old mum was stuffing toilet paper down her top to make her bumps look bigger. A young Allie was standing on the toilet laughing, smoking and sticking out her own bumps, wiggling her hips dancing.

'Mum,' I cried out. 'Mum!' I scrambled up, unlocked my toilet door and ran round to the next cubicle – but it was empty. The door banging in the wind from the open window.

A snigger came from behind me. I jumped round.

Lucy Potts was leaning against the wash basins.

'Talking to yourself, London-girl? Did you think you could hide? You'll be sorry, Grace Wilson,' she said and ran off smirking.

The school bell rang. I crept to the back of

the Year Five line in the corridor waiting to go to Assembly. Robert, who was at the front of the line, saw me and bundled the whole queue backwards so I got trampled on and fell over on my bottom.

Joanna, the small girl with the mousy plaits who had smiled at me the first day Miss Sams had sent me to stand in the corridor, helped me back up to my feet. She stuck her tongue out at Robert's back and gave me half of the Kit Kat she had hidden in her pocket. It was a bit fluffy.

'Grace, Grace!' It was Megan, running down the corridor shouting – her wellies leaving muddy footprints, her black curls tumbling over her face. She reached me, heaving for breath.

'Megan, where have you been?' I cried.

'Our Claude has only gone and run off with Ryan's mobile in his mouth again,' said Megan.

'It's not Claude's fault he thinks it's a toy,' I said.

'I can't find where he's hid it, Grace. I've looked everywhere. That's why I'm so late. Ryan went mental at me 'cause he's going to the market with Mr Bradley, and your stupid grandad hasn't got a mobile 'cause he thinks they're a menace, yet he always gives everyone our Ryan's number in case anyone needs to get hold of him when he's not on the farm. He's so annoying. After the last time it went missing Mr Bradley said Ryan was to never forget his mobile on market day again. Anyroad, Claude and me are in *big, big* trouble.'

'Megan Haggett.' Mr Grantham was marching down the corridor, his glasses bouncing on his nose. 'What are you doing in the Year Five queue talking when you are meant to stand with Year Six in silence? You'll do litter duty this break please,' bellowed Mr Grantham.

I felt sick to my toes. I would be on my own without Megan all break. Robert and Lucy turned round from the front of the queue with cold eyes and gave me a horrible smile.

How would I survive break without Megan?

11

I am writing this in my Special Blue Book in secret on my lap under the desk. I am meant to be doing rubbish sums. Lucy Potts has been sent on an errand by Miss Sams so there is no one to tell tales on me. Ha ha.

I think Miss Sams is suspicious. She keeps looking over at me.

Megan is in big trouble. Litter duty means she has to collect a bin bag from Mr Grantham's office and pick up all the empty crisp bags and chocolate wrappers that are dropped during break. It's not fair AND it's the last day before the Easter holidays. Well, there's less than a day left actually 'cause it's nearly break time.

Whoa! Miss Sams is com—

That was MEGA CLOSE but I hid my Special Blue Book just in time and did my best I-HAVE-BEEN-DOING-MY-SUMS-ALL-THE-TIME FACE.

Miss Sams is writing the story title on the white board that we are going to do in literacy after morning break, it says: Write a story called 'Behind the Door'.

The bell rang. 'Outside everyone!' shouted Miss Sams.

Everyone banged and crashed out to the yard but I decided to stay in the classroom, 'cause there is no way I will be allowed to talk to Megan whilst they are forcing her to pick up all the rubbish in the whole school.

'Hurry up, Grace,' said Miss Sams. 'I am desperate for a cup of coffee. You lot have worn me out.'

'You go, miss, my pen has run out,' I lied. 'I need another one for Literacy.' I pretended to rummage in my purple rucksack.

'Make sure you go out to get some fresh air,' said Miss Sams, falling for my lie and leaving the classroom.

I decided to start writing my story in my Literacy book.

Behind a door that once was blue, in a kingdom far away, lived Princess Chloe and Princess Allie. They couldn't stop dancing. They danced all day and all night and were very happy. At the other side of the kingdom in a big house lived a miserable old goat who put a spell on them and

Then, like a knife cutting my heart, I suddenly missed Mum so badly, and scary thoughts and feelings about lumps started to tumble into my brain, so I stopped writing my story and instead got out my Special Blue Book and wrote:

I WANT MUM. I DO NOT WANT to

'GIVE IT BACK, LUCY POTTS!' I screamed, as she ripped the book from under me. She climbed on top of the tables, waving my Special Blue Book in the air. She opened it and read:

'I want Mum.'

'Ah, do you want your mummy, you baby? Well, she doesn't want you. Catch!' She threw my private Blue Book in the air to Robert, who was standing in the doorway laughing.

I watched, lightning bolts of panic ripping through me as Megan's note and my other special things that were hidden between the pages fluttered to the ground. I scrabbled on my hands and knees to pick them all up.

'What's the matter, London-girl? Don't you want to play? Not very nice, is it, when we are trying to be friends?' said Robert, waving my book around. Behind him stood Hannah and Tom.

'Catch,' said Robert as he jumped up on to a chair and then threw my book to Hannah.

'Are we not good enough for you, London-girl?' said Hannah. 'Didn't want to hang around with us, did you, even though we said you could? You'd rather hang around with minging Megan instead. Not very friendly, is it?' She threw the book to Tom.

'GIVE IT BACK!' I screamed.

'You talk funny,' he said, dangling my Special Blue Book in front of my face. Each time I went to grab it he moved backwards, till we were in the corridor. Then all four of them surrounded me, digging me in my back until they'd shoved me out of the side door next to the 'Mummy and me' picture, two of the drawing pins now on the floor. Robert put them in his pocket and pushed me hard in the back one last time. I flew out, sprawling, into the playground.

Again they crowded around me, pushed me against a wall, and started pinching me and laughing.

'DON'T!' I yelled.

'*DON'T!*' they screamed back, imitating, mocking my voice. Lucy stood at the front, pinching me hardest. Their gawping, drooling, laughing faces swam in front of me. Then smack, my face hit the tarmac.

As I spun down into the dark I felt my mum's arms hugging me, holding me tight, then – blankness . . . Quiet . . . Peace . . .

12

'Grace . . . Grace, can you hear me?

'Blood sisters,' she whispered in my ear. 'Don't die, Grace.'

I felt Megan's arms around me as she helped me to my feet.

One of Megan's red wellies lay in a puddle. The sleeve of her red coat was torn and hung off limply, she had a graze on her cheek and her eye was swelling up. Her black bin bag lay discarded on the ground.

Megan turned to face the bullies, who were standing in a huddle looking scared.

'You stinking cowards. You never go near my friend again. If any of you worms so much as give Grace a dirty look I will make *you* look so stupid you will drop dead of shame. And don't think you will ever be able to sleep at night, 'cause I will come into your dreams and I WILL GET YOU.'

'Megan Haggett, get in my office now!' shouted Mr Grantham as he strode across the playground towards us. 'Fighting and threatening people in the playground! I will not tolerate such behaviour.'

'It wasn't Megan, sir . . .' I began, but the words came out funny. My lip felt like a giant's and I could taste gravel in my mouth.

'Where there's you there's ALWAYS trouble, Megan!' he shouted.

I stepped in front of Megan and tried again. 'Megan didn't do this,' I said, looking the headmaster straight in the eye.

Mr Grantham's chin hit his collar as he looked my cuts and bruises up and down.

'Why do you always blame Megan, sir?' I said.

Megan stepped in front of me. 'I wouldn't hurt our Grace, sir, she's my best friend. You said in Assembly last week that we had to name and shame bullies. So that's what I'm doing, sir. I'm naming and shaming. It's Lucy, Hannah, Tom and Robert who need to go to your office. Look what they've done to her. LOOK WHAT THEY'VE DONE TO MY FRIEND!' screamed Megan.

An angry tear leaked from her eye; she flicked it away like an annoying wasp.

I could feel blood dripping off the end of my nose.

Mr Grantham's body drooped. He looked like he was a thousand years old. He nodded at Lucy, Hannah, Tom and Robert. 'Wait at my desk,' he said. They didn't even try to argue as they scuttled and slithered towards the headmaster's office. Mr Grantham stormed after them. It was then that I spotted my Special Blue Book lying face down in the mud.

I limped over to it and tried to reach down, but my legs wobbled. An arm grabbed me. It was Miss Sams.

'I'll get it, Grace,' she said. She eased it carefully from the mud. Some of the pages were torn and the lovely blue cover was splattered with dirt.

'Oh, miss,' I said. 'Look what they've done.'

'Is this where you write down your special, private thoughts and dreams?' said Miss Sams.

I nodded. 'And my stories and plays, miss,' I whispered.

'I won't look,' she said. 'I'll just clean it up and make it as good as new.'

I felt some spits of rain on my bare arms.

'Come on, girls, let's get you inside.' Miss Sams grabbed Megan's black bin bag in one hand and put my Special Blue Book safely under her arm. She walked behind us as Megan and I did *ouch*, *ouch* wobbly steps across the playground towards the open door.

Kylie gasped and dropped a pile of papers on the floor when she saw us. She helped us into chairs.

'Let's get you cleaned up,' she said.

The door of Mr Grantham's office was shut. As Kylie helped me roll up my jeans to look at my cut knee I could hear Lucy's and Hannah's whining coming through the walls. As she examined our cuts and bruises, Tom's and Robert's lies started to seep under the door. Mr Grantham's voice shook with anger as he started to ooze the truth from them.

Kylie opened the First Aid cupboard and started to rummage through bottles and jars and bandages for what she needed.

There was a knock on the door and Miss Sams hurried in, carrying my jacket and purple rucksack and Megan's school bag. She reached into her pocket and brought out my Special Blue Book.

'I've cleaned it with wet wipes and the dryer in the toilet and mended the pages with Sellotape. I promise I've not peeped at your private words. There you go, as good as new.'

It wasn't quite as good as new, but I gave

her my best I-am-very–grateful-to-you face.

My hip hurt. It was my phone in my pocket sticking into me. I tried to reach for it but my hand was too sore. Miss Sams helped me pull it out. She switched it on to make sure it wasn't broken. A text came through straight away.

B happy. Luv u, Mum xxx.

I shook with sobs; I couldn't stop them. Miss Sams put her arm around my shoulder softly and her gentle voice tickled my ear.

'We will make sure this doesn't happen to you ever again,' she whispered.

Miss Sams knelt on the floor beside Megan and put her hand on her forehead.

'Did you bang your head, Megan?'

'Don't think so, miss. Did this fighting them beasts off our Grace,' she said.

Miss Sams smiled the sweetest of smiles at Megan.

Kylie started to clean under Megan's

eye and the graze on her cheek. Megan didn't even flinch – she kept her eyes tight closed, held completely still till Kylie had finished.

'Blood sisters,' I whispered to her.

She opened her eyes. 'Blood sisters till we die,' she whispered back.

Kylie started dabbing at my knee with something smelly in a bottle. *OUCH*, it stung. My eyes started watering. I wasn't crying any more, honest. Kylie handed me some tissues.

'Write something in that little blue book of yours,' she said. 'And keep writing, no matter what! It will take your mind off it. I've got to get that knee of yours clean.'

Once upon a time in a land far away lived a brave pig called Sir Claude.

'Hold still and keep writing,' said Kylie. 'I've got to get the grit out of that cut.'

Once upon a time in a land far away lived a brave pig call Sir Claude. He was a knight whose life's work was to protect the beautiful dancing Princess Chloe from all the bad lumps that lived in the land. He rode around on his trusty steed (coz that's what they called horses in the olden days).

In the dead of night a bad lump sneaked into the castle and up the winding staircase and into Princess Chloe's bed chamber. It got nearer and nearer to the sleeping princess. But aha! Sir Claude was hiding under the bed to slay the lump. (Slay was the olden-day word for kill.) He got ready to pounce but OH NO, HE WAS STUCK UNDER THE BED! The lump got bigger and bigger and bigger and nearer and nearer to the sleeping Princess Chloe. Then, with an almighty push, Sir Claude sent the giant four-poster bed flying up in the air and freed himself. He caught Princess Chloe with one trotter and slayed the lump with the other . . .

The headmaster's office door banged open. When he saw us, Mr Grantham smiled a kind of friendly dad-type smile. But it didn't work, because he's the headmaster and not my dad.

He marched Robert, Tom, Lucy and Hannah through the office. As they passed us they kept their eyes skating on the grey lino. Lucy stopped and looked back at me and glued my eyes with hate. I pushed myself up from the chair, held my head up high and smiled right back at her.

Lucy didn't have what I had, a best friend like Megan. Robert, Tom and Hannah were stuck to her with bribery and fear, not friendship. Lucy looked confused and scuttled off after the others. Through the window I could see the rain splashing down in the school playground, but as I looked at my best friend the lightning and thunder inside me stopped. The storm became calm as I smiled at Megan.

13

'Grace . . . Grace, wake up, love.' Something tickled my nose. It was the fringe of a shawl. I could hear rain splattering against the window. I forced my eyes open. Allie was leaning over me. She helped me sit up, putting white lace pillows behind me. I wasn't at Grandad's house, but in the big double bed in Allie's room.

I stretched my leg under the white quilt. It was sore. I felt something with my toes and reached down. It was Ryan's mobile phone.

The memories came flooding back into my brain. Grandad was at market with Ryan. No one could contact them 'cause Claude had hidden the phone. Grandad did not know what had happened at school and now I was here in the cottage where I was forbidden to go.

I felt ice in my tummy.

'Claude, you little beggar,' said Megan, as I pulled the phone from the covers. Megan was sitting on the end of the bed cuddling the little pig. 'Is this your new hiding place in me mam's bed? I got into big, big trouble 'cause of you.' And she tickled the little pig on his tummy.

Megan was wearing a huge yellow T-shirt. I looked down at myself. I was in a turquoise one.

'Our Ryan's,' said Megan. 'You fell asleep in Kylie's office and then you were sick all down your clothes. It was gross. Uck! So we brought you back here to look after you.'

Claude squealed and wriggled out of Megan's arms and tried to grab the phone in his teeth, but even though I was sore I moved quickly to pass the phone to Allie.

'Looks like that pig has done you a favour,' laughed Allie. 'We can't phone your grandad, and that means we get to spend some time with you.'

'But Grandad will be so angry,' I said.

'But I think it's what your mum would want,' said Allie as she kissed me on the cheek.

I nodded, feeling scared, but I also felt the tiniest ray of sunshine twinkling in my tummy.

'Claude, thank you,' I said, reaching out for the little pig. I gave him a kiss.

'Can I come in?' The door opened and an old, crinkly, silver-haired man put his head round the door.

'Come in, doctor. Here they are, battered and bruised for you to patch 'em up. We still can't locate her grandad,' said Allie.

Megan looked at me and winked.

'So I've been told,' said the doctor. 'Tommy let me in. He asked me to tell you he's gone to wait for Ryan and Mr Grantham at the end of the lane.'

He turned to me. 'I'm Doctor March,' he said. 'I remember patching up your mum with her bumps and scrapes, many moons ago.' He smiled and shone a little torch in my eyes.

'How many fingers am I holding up?' he asked.

'Three,' I said.

'Eleven,' said Megan.

'Don't be cheeky,' said Doctor March. 'Good.' He put his torch away. 'You'll mend.'

Then he hurt me as he examined my lip, nose and knee.

'You'll have a right shiner in the morning, Megan,' he said as he moved on to examine her. She didn't even flinch.

'They will both need to be watched closely over the next twenty-four hours. Can Grace stay here with you tonight?'

Bang bang bang on the door that once was blue. We all jumped. Claude squealed and hid his face in my lap.

'Hello, is anyone there?' roared a voice.

It was Grandad.

14

Claude dived under the covers, squealing, as Lara bounded into the room, knocking Doctor March over as she landed on the bed. She barked and shook raindrops all over us. I squealed and flung my arms around Lara and Megan, and we buried our faces in her damp golden fur.

'Get down here, you daft dog,' shouted Grandad.

'It's quite all right, Mr Bradley,' I could hear Allie say as she showed Grandad upstairs. 'All animals and people are welcome here.'

Grandad strode into the room.

'Grace,' he said, 'look at me.' I could feel his eyes burning into me so I unburied my face from Lara's coat.

Grandad's eyes changed from shocked to sad to angry in less than a blink as he gazed from me to Megan, then back to me again.

'Been scrapping have you, the pair of you? I told you, no trouble. Come on, let's be having you. Get your things together. We're going home.'

'Mr Bradley,' said Doctor March as he brushed himself down. 'They have not been scrapping. From the sounds of things, young Megan here saved your granddaughter from a baying pack of bullies. She's a brave one and no mistake. Why, man, you should be thanking her, not chiding her! As Grace has bumped her head, I must insist that she stays here for the night so that Mrs Haggett can check on her every hour, which you cannot do as you've cows to milk. If you insist on her going home with you and that daft dog, who's liable to send her flying, *I* shall insist Grace stays at the Royal Middleton Hospital for the night.'

Grandad shrivelled into a burst party balloon.

'Very well . . . Much obliged, I'm sure . . . Make sure you behave, Grace. Mind your Ps and Qs . . . Lara – heel!' He put his hand on my head and left, just like that. I couldn't believe it.

'Shut your mouth, our Grace. You look like a seal waiting for a fish,' laughed Megan.

As Grandad stomped down the stairs Allie whispered, 'Thank you so much, Doctor. You're the only person in the whole village Mr Bradley will listen to.'

'Aye, I always did boss your grandad around,' twinkled the doctor. 'Have a nice evening.'

Lara jumped off the bed and ran up to Allie, putting her paws on her shoulders and licking her cheek.

'Get down, you daft dog,' said Allie. 'Down the stairs with you, go on. Follow your master.'

Lara barked and then the crazy whirlwind of golden fur was gone.

'Lara doesn't know her Ps and Qs,' I said. Megan cracked up laughing.

'She's been expelled from every dog training school in Yorkshire,' said Ryan, sticking his head round the door. 'Look at the pair of you. Who did this to you? I'll—'

'You'll do nothing. School's dealing with it. Go and fetch Kylie, you'll be late for the film,' said Allie, handing him his mobile. 'Doctor March, let me show you out.' And with that, Ryan, Doctor March and Allie clattered down the stairs.

Claude stuck his nose out from under the covers. The phone rang in the hall. I heard Allie answer it.

I needed a wee desperate – like two-seconds-to-spare desperate. I flung the quilt off my legs and swung my feet on to the floor. I did *ouch*, *ouch*, wobbly quick footsteps to the bathroom.

When I came back Megan was sitting on the bed with my phone in her hand. She was reading my texts. Hailstones of anger fizzled in my tummy.

'That's private, Megan. You shouldn't be

looking at my texts.' I tried to snatch the phone back.

But Megan held on to it tight. 'Oh Grace, you should have told me,' she said.

'Those texts were for me, not you,' I shouted.

'I didn't mean to stick my nose in Grace, but your phone bleeped when you were in the toilet, and I got it from your bag, in case it were a text from your mam but . . .'

I tried to grab the phone back again but Megan leaped up on the bed and held my phone high in the air so I couldn't reach. 'I've read 'em all, Grace. All of them nasty bully texts.'

Megan looked down at the phone and read: '*We don't want you in our school. You and Megan are mingers with your ugly hair. Go back to London and take Megan and her minging red wellies with you.*'

I had a major tonsil jam. I tried, but no words would come out. I felt sick to my toes and flopped down on the edge of the bed.

Megan bounced down next to me and the

two of us just sat there, as the world stood still waiting for the words to come.

'Why didn't you tell me?' said Megan after what seemed like years and years. 'I thought we were best friends – blood sisters . . .'

'We are,' I said, 'till we die. But I didn't want their poison words to hurt your feelings, Megan. I didn't want you to read what they called you. You're my best friend on Planet Earth.'

'Do you think I don't know what they say about me? "Smelly" and "minger" and always laughing at my wellies. I used to care but now I don't. They can fling names at me all they like 'cause their words will bounce off me 'cause I've got you as my friend. But you should have told me.' Then she kissed me on the cheek.

The hailstones in my tummy stopped as I gave Megan a hug.

'Are you going to tell?' I asked.

'I am going to wait for the perfect moment, just you see,' said Megan. She gave me back my phone.

Allie appeared with two mugs of steaming

hot chocolate with squirty cream on the top. Megan reached under the bed and brought out an old battered Monopoly board and started to set it up.

'That was Mr Grantham on the phone,' said Allie. 'He excluded the bullies for the rest of the day and they all have to go into school during the Easter break to do extra work. So let's forget about 'em now and have a good time.'

Megan cheered, Claude squealed and ran round the room. I laughed but it hurt my lip.

Monopoly was tricky 'cause Claude kept running off with the money and Megan had to chase him . . . and just for those hours I was in heaven.

That night I woke as moonlight tiptoed on my face. Megan lay snoring beside me. Allie lay sleeping on a mattress at the foot of the bed. I swung my legs on to the floor and winced as my knee brushed the quilt. I peeped through the window, round the deep red curtains, rubbing the velvet against my cheek. I could see Kylie and Ryan snogging in a car.

The rain had stopped. The moonlight danced in the puddles as the shadows jumped and flickered in the farmyard. Out of the corner of my eye I saw something disappear behind the cowshed. Then, there they were: young Mum and Allie dancing in the moonlight, behind the pig pen, around the barn – running and laughing. Martha stalked across the yard. As I watched she became bigger, sleeker, older, and her tabby coat changed to black. '*Penny!*' cried my mum's voice, and she scooped up her cat and held her against her cheek. I ran, sliding down the stairs on my bottom and out through the door that once was blue. In my bare feet I ran and ran, splashing through the puddles towards the laughter, holding my arms out, reaching for my mum.

But she wasn't there.

'Grace?' I turned and Ryan was behind me, taking off his jacket to wrap round me. He grabbed my waist and flung me over his shoulder. Kylie reached out and held my dangling hand. Allie was waiting at the door.

'Were you dancing in the moonlight with the shadows, Grace? Come, let's get you back to bed.'

Something made me glance back at the farmhouse. Grandad was watching me out of the upstairs window.

15

I AM NOT ALLOWED IN THE COTTAGE WITH THE
DOOR THAT ONCE WAS BLUE EVER AGAIN!!!!
ALLIE AND GRANDAD ARE NOT TALKING. <u>IT'S
OFFICIAL</u>.

This morning, Grandad was waiting for me
outside the door of the cottage under an
anger cloud.

'WHAT WAS OUR GRACE DOING, RUNNING
AROUND THE FARMYARD AT NIGHT IN NOUGHT
BUT A T-SHIRT?' he shouted.

'Oh, Mr Bradley,' Allie said, 'haven't you ever wanted
to dance with shadows in the moonlight?'

'No,' he said, 'I can't say as I have. YOU WERE
MEANT TO BE KEEPING AN EYE ON HER. Good
day to you, Mrs Haggett,' and he marched me across

the farmyard and up the stairs to my bedroom, which is where I am now writing this under the bed covers, with the torch from the wellington boot cupboard, even though it is daytime.

Old Goat Grandad has banned me from seeing, talking to, smiling at and breathing the same air as Megan Haggett. Blah blah blah blah blah. IT'S ALL JUST ONE BIG BLAH.

But he forgot texting, ha ha ha.

SISTERS, I texted her.

BLOOD SISTERS TILL WE DIE, my best friend texted back.

Uh-oh, someone is coming . . .

I felt the bed sag as someone heavy sat on the end of it.

'Grace.' It was Grandad. 'Grace, talk to me please. I only want what's best for you.'

I am ignoring him.

'You should have told me you were being bullied, Grace. I could have done something to help.'

I am *still* ignoring him.

'Grace, come on, let's get some fresh air. I will show you my garden. You can plant some flowers if you want. Your mum always loved cornflowers and sweet peas. They were her favourites when she were your age.'

I nearly told Grandad that they still are her favourite flowers. I nearly did but I AM KEEPING REALLY STILL AND QUIET. HOPING OLD GOAT WILL GO AWAY AND LEAVE ME ALONE.

'I'll leave you alone to sleep then, shall I? Let you get some rest.'

He's gone. I WISH GRANDAD WOULD Go

Suddenly the quilt was pulled back, sending the torch flying and jogging my writing. Polly stared down at me.

'Sit up now, young lady, 'cause you are not going to ignore me, I'll tell you that for nought. Your grandad's right upset. He just wants to keep you safe, that's all. Now let's be having you.'

Polly started to take out pots and tubes from her overall pockets and then poured stuff on cotton-wool pads. It stank. She pressed it on my lip before I could argue.

'This is a poultice, my mother's own recipe. Will bring the swelling down in no time it will.'

My lip tingled. Then she put different ointments on my scrapes and bruises.

'Your grandad is trying his best you know,' she said, dabbing too hard at my knee and making me flinch. 'If you know what's good for you, you'll go and join him in the garden once we're done here.'

Grandad was kneeling over a flower bed of cornflowers when I found him. I knelt next to him on my sore knee.

'They are still Mum's favourite,' I said, 'and sweet peas.'

Grandad's eyes almost twinkled. 'Sweet peas won't be out till July.' He started to pick a bunch of cornflowers. 'For your room,' he said. 'So you can think of your mum.'

'I think about her all the time,' I said. 'I never ever stop thinking about her. I miss her.'

'I know, duck,' he said.

'It wasn't Allie's fault. I crept out when she was asleep. I thought I saw . . .'

'You thought you saw your mum,' finished Grandad. 'I think I see her shadow dancing all the time,' he said. 'Behind the pig pen . . .'

'And the cowshed,' I finished. 'But she's not really there.' And I took Grandad's hand, grabbed the bunch of flowers in my other hand and we went in for some tea.

A VERY IMPORTANT PART FROM MY SPECIAL BLUE
BOOK THAT I WILL LET YOU PEEP AT.

I am bored **bored bored** without my best friend.

I still think Grandad's an old goat for not letting
me see Megan, but I think he's very lonely.

For one week I have had every breakfast and lunch
and dinner with Grandad. He tries to find things to say
but he doesn't know how to talk to someone who is
10 years and 11 weeks and 1 day. He just knows
about boring old tractors and crops, but when he
talks about animals I love it, only I don't show it. I
PUT ON MY BEST YOU-WON'T-LET-ME-SEE-MY-
BEST-FRIEND-MEGAN FACE.

After dinner we always phone Mum from Grandad's
phone.

I've not got enough credit to use my purple mobile
to call her. She still sounds weird – her voice is too
bright and shiny and I can't tell her proper stuff coz
GRANDAD IS ALWAYS HOVERING IN THE
BACKGROUND.

It's not like it used to be when we danced round the

house together with the music turned up loud and I brushed her hair and could tell her anything.

I STILL TEXT HER EVERY NIGHT BEFORE I GO TO SLEEP: Hug you.

And she texts back: Hug you more.

I can hear a squealing outside – wait a minute . . .

When I opened the back door there was Claude, his red harness trailing behind him in the mud.

Allie was standing in the farmyard, and she waved to show it was OK for me to pick up the little pig and take him inside. She put her finger on her lips and vanished into the darkness. Sticking out from Claude's harness was this note from Megan.

Please look after Claude. coz I am sad coz I can't c u I am going 2 Blackpool 2 stay with Nana Haggett. They will not let Claude come co z he will do Nana's head in and frighten donkeys on the beach. He has hidden our Ryan's phone again!!!

Text me, blood sister, and give Claude lots of xxxx

I snuck Claude past Grandad, who was talking in a hushed voice to someone on the phone.

I am now in my bedroom writing this and have put Megan's note carefully between the pages of my Special Blue Book.

Grandad is calling me down to the phone to say hello to Mrs Johnson . . .

I shut Claude carefully in my bedroom – Claude got stuck under the bed.

I BANGED MY HEAD PULLING HIM OUT.

He hid my Special Blue Book under Mum's old dusty teenage magazines.

I am sitting on my bed cuddling Claude and writing this at the same time, which is hard.

Mrs Johnson said Mum was still being kept in hospital after her check-up as she was feeling a bit sick and tired, but she thought that Mum would talk to me tomorrow. The scary words and thoughts are tumbling into my brain again.

MUM GOT HER LUMP DANCING

MUM GOT HER LUMP DANC—

I JUST HEARD A TINKLE OF GLASS FROM THE BUTTERFLY MOBILE AND SAW LILAC LIGHT SHOOT ACROSS THE ROOM.

Mum was sitting on the window sill next to the jug of cornflowers. She smiled and leaned over to smell the flowers. Then she just vanished.

Tears keep escaping from my eyes while I'm trying to write and Claude is licking them.

I AM GOING TO GO TO SLEEP NOW SO I DON'T SMUDGE THE INK.

I just texted Mum 'Hug you'. Just in case.

But no text has come back.

16

These are Megan's texts from Blackpool. (I copied them at night-time in secret, under the bed covers by the light of the torch from the wellington boot cupboard.)

Today I went on a donkey. I stood on the donkey's back and balanced like an acrobat. The donkey man told me off. Nana shouted at him. Miss you XX

Wish u were here. I am eating chips and gravy every day. I told Nana that school said we had to eat healthy. Five portions of fruit and veg a day. She said, 'What r u talking about, you daft lass? Chips are potatoes, aren't they?' And she bought me another portion. I love my nan. Miss you XXX

Today I went on the Big Dipper with Nan. She was sick. Then she bought me a candy floss and I was sick. Miss you, my best friend XX

My days are no longer boring. I thought Grandad would kick off about Claude but Ryan shouted across the farmyard to him, 'She can keep the annoying little beggar till our Megan gets back from Blackpool. Do us all a favour,' and he patted his phone in his pocket.

Grandad didn't say anything but later I saw that he had put an old cardboard box with some straw and a blanket inside at the bottom of my bed for Claude to sleep in. He doesn't though. Claude is snuggled up in bed next to me.

CLAUDE IS THE BEST PIG IN THE WORLD. I READ MEGAN'S TEXTS TO CLAUDE. WE BOTH MISS HER LOTS.

Claude keeps trying to grab my pen in his mouth.

Not everyone is happy that Claude has come to stay. Martha hisses and spits at him but when Claude and I chase each other up and down the stairs and in and out of rooms, she follows us at a distance, meowing.

Lara has been banned from my room while Claude is staying. I can sometimes hear her whining and scratching outside the door.

Polly shouted at us this morning: 'Mind my floor, I've just washed it! You and that blessed little pig putting muck about the house, giving me extra work. He's good for nought but sausages.'

I covered Claude's ears but I caught Polly smiling at us when she thought I wasn't looking as she watched us play.

I feel tired now. I THINK I'LL JUST SHUT MY EYES FOR

Crack! A stone clattered against the window. I sat bolt upright in bed. My dreams of lumps and disappearing dads and running over green quilts and leaping over cows and horses to get back to Mum vanished.

Crack! Another stone smashed against the window. My mobile bleeped to say I had a text.

Look outside x

I jumped out of bed. Megan was standing in the dark, waving.

Another text came through.

Ryan and your grandad r in the barn 2night with a sick cow. U r safe 2 come 2 cottage. Meet me at outside bog. Megan xx

I pulled on my jeans, a jumper and a pair of socks and woke Claude and put his red harness on. I grabbed the torch and ran down the stairs with Claude to the scullery and stuffed my feet in the green wellington boots.

Claude and I made our way over the mud bumps to the outside bog. In the light of my torch I saw the toe of a red wellington boot peeping round the corner. There she was, just like the first time we met, my best friend, Megan the rainbow-girl.

Megan put her finger up to her lips and grabbed Claude in her arms, planting kisses all over his face. Then she flung her arms round me and kissed my cheek. Holding hands, we crept down the bumpy path and when we came to the open door of the barn I could see Grandad and Ryan bending over a black-and-white cow that was lying on its side, bellowing.

I held my breath as we passed slowly, step by step.

When we were safely past the barn, we sprinted the short distance to the cottage and through the door that once was blue. I could hear shouting coming from the kitchen. We took our wellies off, crept down the hall and peeped through the gap of the half-open kitchen door.

Allie's eyes were sparking at Tommy. 'I told you to be back from the pub an hour ago.'

'Stop shouting, woman, I were just having a beer at the Pig and Whistle,' yelled Tommy.

'Your dinner is ruined,' screamed Allie. She reached for a plate and tipped it over his head – potatoes, gravy and peas came trickling down Tommy's red nose.

They both glared at each other, then started to laugh and laugh. Allie got a cloth and gently wiped the gravy from Tommy's cheek. She planted a kiss on his lips and he put his arms round her.

'Oh, Tommy, I'm that scared. I just want Chloe—'

Tommy saw me in the doorway and shook Allie to stop her words. Ice trickled into my tummy and my legs wobbled.

Allie turned round and grabbed hold of me. She took me to an armchair and pulled me on to her lap and cuddled me and whispered into my hair, 'What thee needs is cuddles, not manners, whatever your grandad says.'

The feel of her arms round me was more precious than diamonds.

'I'm going to see if they need help with yon cow,' Tommy announced as the cow's bellows shot through the dark. He tottered out of the back door.

'You do that,' said Allie. 'Megan, fetch that over, will you, love?' She nodded to an old tin box that was perched on a shelf.

Megan put the box on the kitchen table and we all sat round as Allie opened it.

'Found these when I had a right good clear out when our Megan were in Blackpool.'

Allie pulled out lots of yellowing photos. One was of her and my mum when they were about five – two little girls, playing in wellies by the outside bog. Another one was when they were about eight, hiding behind the pig pen, with a lady in a green dress with a mop of brown curls, who had her finger over her lips.

'That lady's your grandmother, Grace, just before she ran off with her soldier.'

I stared at the stranger lady who was my

gran. I hated her for leaving my mum and for making my grandad a miserable old goat. I hid that photo at the bottom of the pile.

Allie picked up one of her and my mum at about my age, feeding the lambs. Mum was wearing the yellow dress and their hair was blowing free in the breeze. The photograph was beautiful.

'Here,' she said, handing me the photo. 'Have this for your little blue book.'

I felt myself burning crimson as I gaped at her.

'I've seen you writing about us all, pet.' She winked at me.

Claude *oink*ed for attention and nibbled my sock. I picked him up for a cuddle. There was a knock on the back door. Megan ran to open it. It was Kylie.

'Is Ryan still with that cow?'

Allie nodded.

'It's making a fair racket,' said Kylie, as an extra-loud bellow smacked my ear drums. 'Happy Easter, girls,' she said, reaching down into her bag and giving Megan and I each a small bag of chocolate eggs.

'Thanks, Miss Princeton – I mean, Kylie,' I said, and gave her a kiss on the cheek.

'Ta very much,' said Megan, spitting chocolate everywhere.

An envelope with a picture of a steam train on the front had fallen out of Kylie's bag.

'What's this?' said Megan, picking it up.

'They're tickets. It's meant to be a secret,' Kylie giggled. 'Oh well, you'll know soon enough anyway. The school governors are paying for the whole of Waldon Primary School to go on a trip to the Railway Museum in York for the day. It'll be next week, when you get back to school after the holidays.'

'Lovely,' said Allie. 'I love a trip out. Me and your mam went to the Railway Museum when we were about your age. But, Megan, you're to keep an eye on Grace. I'm not having her on a coach by herself with that Lucy Potts at large. You are to sit on the coach together. Do you understand?'

'Mam, we won't be allowed. I'm in Year Six. I can't sit on the Year Five coach,' said Megan, dribbling chocolate.

'I don't care, you're sitting together. I'll drop Miss Sams a line. And you're not wearing your wellies. It's proper shoes for a trip out. We'll go and buy you some.'

'But, Maaaaaam . . .' whined Megan.

'Shhh! Can you hear anything?' said Allie.

'No,' said Kylie.

'Exactly, the cow's stopped. The vet must be here. You need to get home, Grace. Quick, your grandad will be back at the farmhouse soon. Run!'

Hand in hand, Megan and I left the rickety cottage stuffed full of loving arguments, and inched our way through the dark, towards the back door of the cold lonely farmhouse full of dreams and manners.

Suddenly, Grandad was silhouetted in the doorway of the cowshed and came striding towards us. Megan pulled me behind the pig pen and we crouched down low. My heart was jigging against my ribs as Grandad's footsteps came nearer and nearer. A squealing filled the air.

Claude had escaped and was running towards the barn. Grandad changed direction and strode after him, cursing under his breath.

'That dratted little pest of a beast. We've just got the cow quiet. That pig'll wake the whole of Yorkshire.'

'I'll distract your grandad,' whispered Megan. 'When you get the chance, *run*!'

Megan charged towards the barn, shouting, 'CLAUDE, GET BACK HERE!'

Grandad had caught Claude and turned to face Megan, still under his anger cloud.

'Sorry, Mr Bradley, sir,' said Megan. 'Claude must have known that I was home from Blackpool and escaped all the way from your Grace's room when she was fast asleep to find me. He's a very clever pig. Can I have him back please, Mr Bradley, sir?'

I heard Grandad start to shout and I took my chance and ran.

'What are you *blah blah blah* at this time of night *blah blah blah* running around screaming *BLAH* PIG *BLAH BLAH* BLAH . . .'

Claude had saved us. I ran to the back door, up all the stairs and along the dark corridor to my room. I switched on the light and the butterfly mobile twinkled, sending orange rays across the room that dazzled my eyes. Through the haze of golden droplets I could see my teenage mum sitting there, so pretty in her swirly swirly dress of pink silk, perched on the window sill, her small bumps starting to show, filling the dress – not like when I had tried it and the dress had flapped in folds round my flat chest. She was holding her arms out to me and smiling. I ran to hug her. But she wasn't there.

I heard Grandad coming up the stairs so I quickly switched off the light and jumped into bed with my clothes still on. He opened the door.

'Grace . . . Grace, are you awake?'

I pulled the covers tight round me, sat up,

and did my best I've-been-asleep-all-night sleepy face.

'What is it, Grandad?' I said.

'Claude escaped but he's back with Megan. Well . . . um . . . I just didn't want you to fret if you woke up and found him gone.'

'Thanks, Grandad,' I said. 'Goodnight.'

'Goodnight, Grace.' And he leaned down and actually kissed my forehead. His lips felt dry and cold, but it gave me sunshine in my tummy.

As soon as he'd shut the door I texted Megan.

I am safe. Pretended to zzzzz when Grandad came in. Lol. U r the best friend in the world. Thanx for that. U saved my life.

My phone beeped.

Any time, blood sister. Thank u 4 looking after Claude. Sleep tight. A x and an oink.

17

I rolled over in bed and stretched my arms out to cuddle Claude, but there was just empty space. Then, *bang*, my memory clicked in. Megan was back from Blackpool, Claude was back at the cottage, and Grandad had nearly caught me last night when I had sneaked out to meet her. It was Easter Sunday. I leaped out of bed.

I wondered if Grandad had bought me an egg. My tummy rumbled for chocolate. I ran out of the bedroom and along the corridor, but as I put my foot on the first stair I looked down and saw mud on the bottom of my jeans. I was still wearing my clothes from last night.

I raced back to my bedroom and tore them

off, rummaging in the wardrobe for a clean pair of jeans, my heart jigging against my ribs. What if Grandad had seen the mud? He would have totally guessed that I had been with Megan out on the farm last night. My insides cartwheeled at the thought of my near mistake. As I pulled up the new jeans my mouth was watering again for chocolate, chocolate, chocolate.

I raced downstairs to breakfast. As I flung the door open I stopped in my tracks. The whole table in front of me was covered with Easter eggs – big eggs, small eggs, miniature chocolate eggs – laid out on the table in lines like soldiers on parade. My grandad was surveying them proudly, like a general inspecting his troops. I forced my legs forward. I read the labels.

Happy Easter from Mrs Green

'The cowman's wife,' said Grandad.

'*Love from Maisy who collects the eggs,*' I read.

Happy Easter from Polly

From Sarah xxx (Polly's daughter)

With love from Margaret (Polly's Mother) xx

Love Nancy and Cliff (Polly's brother and his wife)

It went on and on and on. It seemed like the whole village had sent me eggs. Chocolate from people I didn't even know. A room full of chocolate. Chocolate from strangers who felt sorry for me.

My tummy dropped like an avalanche. The scary words from the computer screen tumbled into my head. 'Mum got her lump dancing,' I whispered, but it didn't work.

The words cut into my brain and spun before my eyes. The hushed telephone conversations, those whispers that stopped when I walked into the room, Allie's half-finished sentence last night.

I closed my eyes and chanted: 'Mum got her

lump dancing. Mum got her lump dancing . . .'

But it still didn't work. My head was telling me that my mum was seriously ill. That this wasn't just a little lump that needed cutting out.

I, Grace Wilson, was a horrible person. I hadn't even thanked her properly for my lovely purple phone.

I counted all the days I had been horrible.

That day when I had slammed the phone down on her without even saying, 'Hug you.'

That day when I hugged her goodbye and walked down the path. I should have turned and looked at her one more time. I knew she was waving, waiting for me to look round. But I didn't. I'd just kept on walking. Why hadn't I ran and hugged her and never ever let her go? Not ever. Why hadn't I looked at her one more time? Why? Why? Why?

Hailstones of anger at myself fizzled in my tummy.

'Come on, Grace, sit down and have some breakfast. Then you will write a thank you letter to all the kind people who have sent you chocolate.'

But I just stood there and looked at him with a hurricane in my head. I found myself screaming, only the scream seemed a long way away, as far away as London, as far away as my mum. The scream became words.

'No, I will not say thank you, I do not want chocolate from strangers. I WANT MY MUM,' I screeched.

Grandad held out his arms to hug me but I pushed past him.

'I don't want to be here with you, Grandad. I want to be with Megan. I'm going to see her – and you can't stop me.'

'Grace, come here. Please stay with me.'

Grandad reached out his arms to hug me again, but I pushed him away and, scooping as many Easter eggs in my arms as I could carry, I ran through the back door in my bare feet, slipping and sliding through the mud, the stones cutting my toes. I ran across the farmyard to the door that once was blue and hammered on it.

Megan opened it, took one look at me and hauled her red wellies on to my feet, only they wouldn't go on properly. She pushed her feet into a giant pair of Ryan's old trainers and we flapped with our clown feet to the outside bog. Megan's arms were round me, hugging me, kissing my tears.

'You've got a right regular feast there, our Grace. We'll not be needing our dinner,' she laughed.

We fell on the eggs, ripping them open, smearing chocolate over our faces, dribbling Smarties and Chocolate Buttons, and then we were both sick together behind the cowshed, the way best friends forever are.

There was one egg left, a lonely forgotten soldier, leaning against the outside bog wall. It was a Quality Street egg. I snatched it up.

'This one is for my mum. I'm going to give it to her today. It will make her feel better.'

'How? You can't just run away,' said Megan.

'I can. I've got to see her, Megan, and you can't stop me.'

'But how are you going to get to London? Get in a stranger's car and end up dead on the front page of the papers? Don't be stupid,' yelled Megan.

'I didn't even turn and wave when I said goodbye to her,' I shouted. 'I have to go.'

'I'm coming with you then,' said Megan. 'But, listen, I've got a plan. If we go today we'll not get far, they'll notice too soon and catch us. But next week's school trip will be perfect. That's when we'll escape.'

MY TOP SECRET RUNAWAY PLAN

It is 3 days till I RUN AWAY with Megan to find Mum.

I have packed and unpacked my purple rucksack 100 times.

These are the important things I am taking with me:

Special Blue Book

IPod

Yellow dress (Mum's) Pink dress (Mum's) A jumper

Torch (from the wellington boot cupboard)

All the Easter eggs that were left on the table. (These will not fit in my rucksack so I have stolen one of Polly's big plastic bags.)

I have hidden my purple rucksack and the plastic bag full of Easter eggs under the bed.

When I talked to Mum on the telephone just now I didn't chat for long coz I don't want any more lies about 'just a little operation'. I am not going to talk to her till I see her and find out the truth. I will just text her lots of 'HUG YOU's until then.

I thought Grandad would actually explode about Easter Day and my screaming fit but he just looked really sad and kept trying to find ways to make me smile.

He watched *The Simpsons* with me.

He put a funny hat on.

He even got Lara to do a mad dog dance. (Grandad said she learned how to do this at dog training school before they chucked her out.)

<u>BUT I WILL NOT SMILE AT HIM.</u>

TWO DAYS LEFT UNTIL OUR ESCAPE TO LONDON.

SCHOOL STARTS TODAY.

Grandad said that I can walk to school alone this term now that I know the way. He even bought me £10 credit for my phone and said, 'Here you go, Grace. Any more trouble from bullies and you call me straight away, do you hear?'

But I don't have to worry coz Lucy, Robert, Tom and Hannah scuttle away from Megan and me whenever they see us coming. Ha ha ha.

I do not sit next to Lucy Potts any more.

Miss Sams has put me next to Joanna. She's the

very small girl with mousey plaits who helped me back on my feet when Robert bundled the Assembly queue backwards. I think she would make a nice friend if I was not running away forever.

ONE DAY LEFT UNTIL OUR ESCAPE TO LONDON. ⭐

My heart is jigging so hard against my ribs I think Lara can hear it. She is following me everywhere. I have unpacked and packed my rucksack one last time to make sure I have got everything.

Megan does not have to hide in the tree and wait for Grandad to go now that I walk to school alone. Instead, she texts me when she is about to leave and I wait a few minutes so that I am behind her. Then she hides behind a bush on the way to school and we walk the rest of the way together, my blood sister and I. But tomorrow we are leaving at 6 in the morning for the SCHOOL TRIP. Grandad will be busy with the cows so Megan and I are walking all the way together.

Ha ha – Grandad will never keep us apart.

Best friends forever.

18

It was still dark when I was woken on runaway day by Martha purring. She was sitting on my pillow, so I buried my face in her fur and gave her a last goodbye kiss. Climbing out of bed, I tiptoed across the room and felt for the light switch.

After I'd thrown on my clothes, I pulled my purple rucksack and plastic bag full of Easter eggs from under the bed. Then I ran downstairs and opened the fridge. Polly had made me a packed lunch of cheese and pickle sandwiches. I shoved the lunch box in my purple rucksack. Lara padded out of her basket and held her paw out to me and started to whine. I knelt down and gave her a goodbye hug. I filled a water bottle for our survival provisions. Lara jumped up, knocking me over, so I gave her a big slice of chicken from the fridge to keep her happy while I sneaked out of the back door.

I could hear Grandad in the cowshed shouting orders over the loud moos of the cows and the sound of machinery pumping and sucking.

I texted Megan. **R u ready?**

On the other side of the yard, the door that had once been blue opened. Megan crept out, wearing her new shoes and carrying a big yellow bag. Under her red coat she was carrying Claude, his nose peeping out between the buttons.

She skidded and slid over the mud bumps and handed me the little pig.

'Claude's coming too. I'm not leaving him. Our Ryan was having a bath last night and Claude jumped in with him. There was this huge howl and our Ryan came running downstairs in nothing but a towel, yelling and screaming, carrying on like a big girl's blouse, said he was going to have Claude-flavoured sausages for his tea.'

'Of course Claude must come,' I said, giggling and giving the little pig a kiss.

Megan changed back into her wellies, throwing her new shoes into the yellow bag and pulling out Claude's harness.

We made our way down the winding lanes to school, Claude scampering beside us on his lead.

The coaches were already there waiting.

Quickly, Megan put Claude in the yellow bag, leaving the zip a bit open so he could breathe. She popped in an apple to keep him quiet.

Miss Sams smiled. 'You two have a lot of bags! We are only going for the day, you know.'

'Our Ryan loves trains, miss. Brought this big bag so I can buy him lots of stuff from the museum shop.'

'I see!' Miss Sams laughed. 'Oh, and I got your mum's letter, Megan. You're fine to go in our coach with Grace. You can help me keep all Year Five in order.'

'We'll have a good old sing-song on the journey, miss,' said Megan as she winked at me.

A silver car stopped outside the school and Lucy Potts got out. She had obviously seen Megan and me and started walking in the opposite direction.

'Quick, Grace, give us your phone and that little blue book of yours,' whispered Megan.

'Megan, they're my private things,' I said, clutching my bag to me.

'I'm not going to be nosey. Give them to me. Trust me. Quick,' said Megan.

I groped in my bag and shoved them in Megan's hand. Then Megan grabbed me by the wrist and screamed at the top of her voice, 'Lucy, my friend, how lovely to see you.' Letting go of me, she ran towards Lucy with her arms out as if she were going to hug her, but instead pulled her behind the back of the coach. I followed, puzzled as to what on earth Megan was up to.

Megan pinned Lucy against the side of the coach and waved my phone in front of her face.

'Oh, look, Lucy, someone has sent Grace a bullying text.'

Megan pressed the phone and read:

'*Your mum couldn't stand the sight of your ugly face, that's why she dumped you here*. I think whoever sent this could get chucked out of school for sending a text like that. I wonder who it's from?' Megan pressed the ring icon on my touch screen. A ring tone came from Lucy's sparkly pink bag.

Lucy looked sick.

'Now listen, you snivelling little bully – we have all the texts. In fact, everything you have ever said to our Grace is written down in this blue book. If you don't do exactly as we say, the book and the phone are going straight to Mr Grantham. Do you understand?'

Lucy nodded.

Megan opened the yellow bag and Claude stuck his nose out. Lucy screamed. Megan put her hand over Lucy's mouth.

'Lucy, shut up. Miss Sams mustn't know about Claude.'

Megan pulled an Easter egg from my carrier bag.

'This is for you, Lucy.'

Lucy looked shocked but still grabbed the egg.

'I want you to get all the people in your class that will keep their mouths shut for chocolate and get them all here now. Go!'

Lucy ran off and in a few minutes she'd brought half the class round the back of the coach, including Hannah, Tom and Robert.

'Line up and open your lunch boxes,' ordered Megan.

They did as they were told. Megan went down the line taking out all the fruit for Claude, and I followed, replacing the fruit with Twixes, Mars bars and Milky Ways from the inside of the eggs. Joanna – my would-have-been friend – peeped round the corner of the coach and waved at me, her mousey plaits bouncing.

I ran up to her and gave her some Kit Kats

and a miniature chocolate egg. Claude *oink*ed loudly.

'Right, you lot,' Megan addressed the line-up of kids, 'every time Claude squeals, you are to sing as loudly as you can so Miss Sams don't catch him. Do you understand?'

'Yes, Megan,' they chorused.

I could hear Miss Sams shouting from the other side of the coach. 'On you get, everyone,' she said loudly, clapping her hands.

Lucy's group barged to the back of the coach, saving places for me and Megan. I sat in the aisle seat so I could keep a lookout for Miss Sams.

The engine rumbled and the coach started to move out of the school gate. Claude squealed and the raucous singing started, covering up the oinks and squeals of pleasure as Claude gulped his fruit down. Tipping my packed lunch into my carrier bag, I emptied some water into the plastic lunch box and held it out for Claude. The little pig lapped it up, splashing water everywhere.

165

For hours we all sang and sang and sang. As the walls of York came into view the whole coach cheered and Claude pressed his nose against the window, squealing in excitement. And so the singing became shouting as we stopped outside the Railway Museum. My heart jigged against my rib-cage. Our time of escape was near.

19

Everyone pushed and shoved to get out of the coach. Megan and I got squashed in the middle of the scrum that rushed to get past Miss Sams.

'Can I have a word please, Megan?' she said as we passed her.

My heart stopped. Megan quickly shoved the bag that hid Claude into my arms.

'What, miss?' asked Megan with wide open eyes, doing her best I-am-innocent-and-am-not-hiding-a-pig face.

'I just wanted to say thanks for keeping everyone entertained,' laughed Miss Sams.

'That's all right, miss, I love singing,' said Megan.

My heart started beating again. I stumbled

off the coach with all my bags and the hidden Claude, who was starting to wriggle.

More coaches parked on either side of us. The one nearest me had a grubby cardboard sign displayed in the window with *London* printed on it.

'Megan, look,' I whispered, pointing to the sign. My brain started to tick.

Loads of shouting, sprawling boys, mostly dressed in jeans and hoodies, tumbled out. A group of four boys stood apart from the others. They looked at Megan's wellies and laughed.

'All right, country-girl,' yelled a tall black boy of about thirteen with this intricate swirly pattern shaved into his short cropped hair. He must have felt my eyes taking in his hairstyle 'cause he turned round and waved at me.

'Tyler,' yelled a boy with ginger spiky hair and lots of freckles, pouncing on him from behind. A pretend punch-up started.

'Tyler and Zack, PACK IT IN!' screamed a teacher's voice hidden behind the heaving, boisterous mob of boys.

The four boys disappeared round the back of their coach.

Miss Sams' attention was on the other two coaches from our school that were driving into the car park.

I pulled Megan away from everyone. 'Quick,' I said. 'While Miss Sams isn't looking, I think we should try to talk to those boys. If they are going home today they might be able to help us get back to London.'

We ran, my carrier bag of Easter eggs banging against my legs. Oinks and squeals were coming from the yellow bag.

'Claude will need to do his business, he must be busting,' puffed Megan.

As we hurtled round the back of the coach we bumped into three of the boys. They were having a spitting competition, seeing who could hit a Coke can. The ginger-haired boy yelled, 'Oy, watch yourself, country-girl. Have you brought your cows?'

'No, but I've got a pig,' laughed Megan, as she lifted Claude out and put his harness on.

The boys' mouths fell open and they all started taking photos of Claude on their phones. I took Claude to a patch of grass to have a wee, double-daring myself to ask the boys if they could help us. A skinny blond boy with dimples came forward to pat Claude, and tripped over the foot that Zack had stuck out deliberately. They all laughed.

'Kyle, man, you fool,' said Tyler.

Megan helped him up.

I forced up all my courage. 'I-I'm G-Grace,' I stammered. 'And this is Megan.'

'You're not a country-girl, are ya?' said Tyler. 'What ends you from?'

'North London,' I said. 'Southgate.'

'We're south. Brockley,' said Zack.

'When are you going back to London?' I asked.

'Today, after we've been to this railway museum,' said Kyle.

'Mitchell, is it still all clear?' yelled Tyler.

Peering round the side of the coach with his back to us was a small black boy with hundreds of tiny plaits that fell to his shoulders. He turned round and gave a thumbs up. He had a round face and the saddest eyes I had ever seen. I smiled at him; he stared at me for a second, then turned round quickly and carried on looking out for their teacher.

The spitting competition started up again.

'Please,' I said, 'I want to ask . . . umm . . . We need to get—'

'Shhh, it's the final,' said Kyle. 'If you're going to watch, you'll have to keep your mouth shut.'

'I'll get their attention,' whispered Megan. 'Watch me.'

So all I could do was stand on the side with Claude as a spectator, itching for the moment to come when I could ask for their help.

Kyle spat and missed the Coke can by miles. Zack was nearer. Then it was Tyler's turn. He missed by a few centimetres. Megan marched straight up and hit the Coke can dead on . . . *Clang.*

'Respect, country-girl,' said Tyler, holding his hand up for a high-five. Megan slapped it, grinning.

'Please,' I said. 'Can you hel—'

'Miss is coming!' yelled Mitchell. 'And there's a lady with red hair following her.'

I quickly lifted Claude back into the yellow bag.

A worried-looking bony woman came round the back of the coach and screamed at the boys. 'Get in the museum NOW!'

The boys pulled their hoods up and did their trying-to-be-cool lolloping walk after their teacher.

'Megan, Grace – what are you doing here?' Miss Sams shouted.

'Sorry, miss,' said Megan. 'Grace thought she had lost her purse. We came round here to empty the things from her bag on to the grass.'

'Found it, miss. It had slipped to the bottom,' I added.

'Quick – we're about to go inside the museum,' said Miss Sams.

We hurried to join the others. We went through the gate and stood in a group with our class. I kept looking and looking for the boys through the crowds of people surrounding us till I felt dizzy, but they were nowhere to be seen. I had to find them.

Miss Sams counted us and gave Megan and me a pile of papers to hand out to the others.

It said:

Find a train and imagine you are a passenger on that train. How would you be dressed and where are you travelling to and why?

Before we could do anything, Miss Sams started her lecture.

'I am trusting you to represent Waldon Primary School and behave yourselves so that we will be invited back in the future. Do you all understand?' *Blah blah blah blah blah.*

'Yes, Miss Sams,' we all chanted. I felt a pin-prick of guilt. It didn't last long. I wanted my mum.

She led us through the gift shop and down the stairs to the Great Hall. My heart stopped as giant engines towered above me – red, green, black – their shining metal funnels reaching towards the sky.

I saw a queue of people behind a big wooden door with a sign on it advertising train rides. At the front of the line stood Zack and Tyler.

'Look, two of the boys are over there. This way,' I said, pulling Megan towards the queue. But just then the door was opened by a bearded man in a guard's uniform and Zack and Tyler disappeared. Just as we reached the door it swung shut.

We pushed open the heavy door and there in front of us on the track stood a black steam train. The engine was stoking up and the chugging sounds and *whoo-whoo*s were deafening. From its funnel, clouds of black smoke filled the air. And in the smoke, my eleven-year-old mum and Allie were holding hands and dancing. Allie was puffing on a cigarette, its smoke becoming the cloud above the steam train. They laughed and ran to one of the carriages.

I grabbed Megan's hand and ran after them, but when I climbed into the carriage it was empty.

'Are you OK, Grace?' said Megan, giving me a hug.

'Yes, it's just I thought I saw . . . It's nothing. I'm fine,' I said.

I stuck my head out of the window to see if I could spy Zack and Tyler. I saw them at the front of the train, being helped up into the engine by the old bearded train guard. Megan and I waved and shouted at them but they didn't see or hear us.

No one else got on our carriage, so as the train started to move we let Claude out. He sat on my knee and stuck his head out of the window, squealing with excitement.

The train chugged around a short track then ground to a halt back at the museum entrance. Putting Claude back in the bag, I jumped down, pulling Megan after me towards the front of the train, trying to reach Zack and Tyler. But as the boys jumped down from the engine ahead of us, their bony teacher was waiting for them with a frown on her face. She marched them back into the museum and they disappeared.

'It's hopeless, Megan. How are we going to get to London?' Lightning bolts of panic shot through me.

'We will find a way to escape. I make a vow to you, my blood sister. I think we should look for somewhere we can hide so that no one will find us. But while we're looking, we've got to do our museum task, finding a train and imagining we are a passenger on it, or Miss Sams will get suspicious,' said Megan.

I nodded and touched my elbow to her hand.

We ran past the old royal carriages that had carpets and sofas and even a bath, and went smack into Lucy Potts – who was standing next to a wax model of Queen Victoria. She was pretending to be her, with Hannah, Robert and Tom curtsying as her servants.

'Your Majesty,' said Megan, and we both curtsied and ran off laughing.

'What about this one?' I said, seeing a dark

green engine with light green stripes and a red trim. 'Look, it says it went on a ship across the Channel to France.'

We ran up the metal staircase to see inside the engine. I was looking at the shiny brass levers and wheels and tried to imagine being a poor stowaway called Claudette, hiding in the train all the way to France so that she could find her long-lost mother. Claudette was really a princess, but did not know it yet. I was just thinking how it would be a brilliant play to write in my Special Blue Book when I saw some old sacking on the floor of the engine.

'Look, Megan, we could hide under there till night-time, when everyone's gone, and then escape back to London.'

'I need to create a diversion,' hissed Megan. 'Look after Claude. Watch.'

Megan jumped down the metal staircase, crept up behind Lucy Potts and gave the wax model of Queen Victoria a push. It wobbled and toppled and fell on top of Lucy Potts, who collapsed backwards. Her legs flailed in the air, showing everyone her pink knickers. Then an alarm went off and staff came running from every corner of the museum.

Megan sprinted back to me and jumped up the metal steps. 'Quick,' she said. She looked around to make sure no one was watching and climbed over the barrier. I handed her the yellow bag with Claude in, my purple rucksack and the carrier of Easter eggs, then Megan helped me over. We landed in a heap on the sacking.

'Ouch!' came from under the sacking.

'Get off!'

'You're squashing me!'

'That's my arm!'

'You're hurting me!'

We quickly crawled off and sat huddled on a bare patch of floor under the steering wheel. I grabbed on to Megan's arm as the sacking moved and the faces of Tyler, Zack, Mitchell and Kyle peeped over the top.

20

'Oh, it's you, country-girl. You're going to have to move. This is our hiding place,' said Tyler.

'And our sacking,' added Zack. 'We took it from the "Do not touch" railway packaging display.'

'Yes, you've got to go now,' said Kyle.

'Do you want some chocolate?' said Megan.

I pulled two Easter eggs out of the bag.

'All right then,' said Tyler and the boys fell upon the chocolate like those starving hyenas on the nature documentaries that my dad used to watch.

'You got to let them stay now,' said Mitchell.

'It's only fair,' mumbled Kyle.

I lifted Claude out of the bag and we all

scratched his tummy as he rolled around on the sacking. I tipped the rest of the water into my lunch box for the little pig. He splashed us as he guzzled.

'So why are you hiding?' I asked the London-boys.

''Cause old Sugdon, the head, has said, that 'cause of Zack's and my behaviour on this trip, we are going to be old men before we'll be allowed to play on the school football team again,' said Tyler.

'Yeah, geriatrics,' said Zack.

'Pensioners,' mumbled Kyle.

'He's just exaggerating the whole situation, right, just 'cause Miss Bailey had to leave the trip halfway through to go on extended leave 'cause of stress. And old Elbows – that's what we calls Miss Ranley, the skinny one you saw moaning at us – has been writing everything we've done down in a book. Can you believe that?' said Tyler.

'Only I robbed her old book from her room,' boasted Kyle.

'You should see the lies what she wrote about us,' huffed Zack.

'So obviously there's no point to school without football,' said Tyler.

'None at all,' said Zack. 'Our coach is leaving soon to get back to London, but Tyler and I are going to stay here in Yorkshire.'

'We are going to get ourselves signed by a football team up here and get rich,' said Tyler.

'You're thirteen, Tyler – and Zack, you're only twelve,' said Mitchell, rolling his eyes.

'Durr, so we add a few years,' said Tyler. 'What's your problem?'

'Can we be you?' I blurted out.

Everyone turned to look at me.

'Can we swap places with you? I'm being serious. Can we have your hoodies to disguise ourselves as boys and get on the coach instead of you? My mum's ill. She's . . .' And the scary words bit into my brain but I couldn't say them. I pushed and kicked them back out again. 'I need to get to London to see her. Please?'

Mitchell was looking straight at me, staring

right into my eyes like he knew . . . Like he could see the scary words.

'I think we should help them,' said Mitchell. 'She's got to see her mum.'

'But Elbows knows us,' said Tyler. 'She says our faces are engraved on her forever. Giving her nightmares.'

'No, it will work,' insisted Mitchell, giving my arm a squeeze. 'I heard old Brownlow say that Elbows could go home on the other coach to have a rest from us.'

'Mr Brownlow's the supply teacher they sent up when Miss Bailey got ill,' explained Kyle. 'He don't know faces, only numbers. He keeps counting us like a mentalist.'

A man walked past shouting, 'Brunswick Boys' School on the coach please,' clapping his hands to get attention.

'Quick,' said Tyler. He gave me his hoodie and Zack gave his to Megan.

'You got to lose your wellies, country-girl,' said Tyler.

'Here,' said Mitchell. He crawled over to his

bag and pulled out an old pair of trainers with a baseball cap. He pulled an elastic band from his pocket and helped Megan put her wild curls in a ponytail and tuck it into the cap. Tyler and Kyle, bent double so as not to be seen over the side of the engine, each pulled off one of Megan's wellies and helped her squash her feet into Mitchell's trainers. We stuffed Megan's red coat and my jacket with the wellies into the bottom of the yellow bag, and the empty lunch box into my carrier bag.

'It's a good thing you're both wearing jeans,' said Mitchell, inspecting his handiwork. 'We'd be in trouble if you was wearing dresses.' We all laughed.

'Shhhh,' said Mitchell, sticking his head out of the engine.

'Now!' he said.

'Good luck, you two,' I whispered to Tyler and Zack. 'I hope you both become famous footballers.'

Tyler winked at me.

Megan lifted Claude back into her bag on top

of the wellies and jackets and leaped over the barrier. Mitchell lifted me over. We climbed down the metal steps to the floor of the museum.

Then we walked in a line, Mitchell on the end, holding my carrier bag, then me with my purple rucksack, then Megan with Claude in the yellow bag, and on the other side was Kyle. We copied their lolloping walks and headed to the coach.

'Hoods down, gentlemen, please,' said the man who I assumed must be Mr Brownlow, as he was counting madly.

'Yes, sir,' we chorused, ignoring him and climbing on the coach.

Megan and I found empty seats together, on the left-hand side near the back, behind Mitchell and Kyle. We squashed ourselves into them. Megan sat by the window, with Claude in his yellow bag balanced on her knee.

Mitchell looked over the back of his seat and reached into my carrier bag. He brought out a bag of tiny chocolate eggs and put his finger to his lips, signalling to the boys sitting near us, pointing as Claude's nose peeped out of the gap in the zip. He then pointed to us and dished out chocolate eggs to all the boys sitting near. There were a few snorts of laughter.

'They won't grass us up,' he whispered. 'Turn your mobiles off so you can't be traced.' I rooted through my bag to find mine. Megan had hers in her pocket. We looked at each other as we pressed our off buttons at the same time.

The coach engine started. Mr Brownlow did one last count and the coach drove out of the car park. I knew there was no turning back now. I looked through the back window. I could see Miss Sams running round the car park. She looked like she was crying.

We soon passed the stone towers and walls of York. We had done it. A cyclone mix of relief, joy and terror whirled through me. We were heading to London.

21

I woke with a jolt. Mitchell was kneeling up on his seat in front of me, his elbows on the backrest, watching me. I smiled.

'I needed to make sure your hoods didn't fall off when you was sleeping,' he said. 'Sir keeps coming down here chatting to everyone about what history they learned in York. He's a right pain. We'd better . . .' He nodded at Megan.

She was fast asleep next to me. Her cheek was flattened against the window. A few of her curls had escaped from her hood. From the yellow bag came tiny little pig snores. Mitchell and I set to work gently tucking her curls back in the hood, trying not to wake her.

He nodded to the empty seat next to him by

the window. Mitchell stood up so I could climb into it.

'Where's Kyle?' I asked.

Mitchell laughed. 'He's keeping sir occupied to stop him wandering down here all the time. He's taken this massive book on steam engines what he got from the gift shop and he's making old Brownlow tell him about every page. I went to check it out. Sir looks like he's got a right headache.'

I looked at Mitchell. He looked so tired. A few of his plaits had worked themselves loose.

'Can I?' I asked, reaching out for his hair.

Mitchell nodded. 'Yeah, my hair's messed up.'

'Why are you doing all this for us?' I asked, as I weaved his hair tightly in and out with my fingers.

Mitchell looked down at his feet.

'Go on, tell me why,' I said again.

Mitchell still wouldn't look at me. I took his chin in my hand and turned his face to me.

'My mum died,' said Mitchell, 'last year. She got cancer.'

Fear danced in my throat at his words.

'I never got to say goodbye 'cause I was at school. I miss her more and more every day. Sometimes I can't breathe I miss her so much. I would do anything just to have one more moment with her but I can't, and I think you should be with your mum. There, I've said it.'

'I see Mum all the time,' I said.

'So do I,' said Mitchell.

'Dancing in smoke,' I said.

'In the winter fire, in the clouds,' said Mitchell.

'Sitting on the window sill – and I go to hug her but . . .'

'She's not there,' finished Mitchell. 'Most of all I see my mum telling me off when I'm in detention with Sugdon.' He laughed.

'Look,' said Mitchell, 'I'm in detention for life when all this comes out, so . . . um . . . could I have your number? Then I can text you to see if you got to see your mum? I wouldn't mind detention so much if I knew you'd made it. That you were with her. That all this was worth it.'

'Course,' I said and keyed my number into his phone.

'Who do you live with?' I asked.

'My dad. Look, my mum wouldn't have approved of you running away but she would have wanted me to make sure you were safe. She'd want me to give you this.' He took twenty pounds out of his pocket. 'There, take it.'

'Thanks,' I said, feeling choked. I didn't know what else to say. I knelt up and reached over to my rucksack on my seat behind and tucked the money into my purple purse in the front pocket.

'What was your mum's name?' I asked.

'Sofia,' he said.

'Sofia,' I said, and I took hold of his hand, and there we sat in understanding.

Kyle came bounding to the back. I dropped Mitchell's hand and climbed back into my seat.

Megan woke up and yawned. 'Where are we?'

'The driver reckons we'll be back in London in about forty-five minutes,' said Kyle.

'Look, I heard sir tell the driver that we are going to stop in Trafalgar Square – he thought it would be a nice way to end the trip and give us a chance to stretch our legs before we head south.'

'That's better for you, isn't it?' said Mitchell. 'That's your best chance to escape.'

'Do you know your way home from there?' asked Megan.

I nodded. Mum had taken me to a lot of musicals and we would often walk down to Trafalgar Square afterwards to see the fountains, before walking back up to Leicester Square station and heading home on the Piccadilly line.

'Kyle, you and I will have a punch-up so that sir is distracted, and then you two can leg it. OK?' said Mitchell.

'Make it a good punch-up,' said Megan, smiling.

'Your mum will be at home, won't she?' said Mitchell.

'Yes, she should be. She's just having checkups every week at the hospital but she comes home at night,' I said.

Claude woke with a tiny snuffle.

'I got him this,' said Kyle, pulling out of his pocket a battered half-full water bottle. 'I made everyone give me what water they had left.'

I reached into my carrier for the lunch box and Kyle poured the water in. The little pig lapped it up.

'We are going to have to find something for Claude to eat, too,' said Megan.

I nodded, and a rainstorm of nerves tingled through me. We were getting nearer.

'We need to be first off the coach so we can start our punch-up,' said Mitchell.

Kyle nodded. 'Bye, you two, nice knowing you,' he said, scratching Claude under his chin. With that, Kyle got his steam engine book and threw it down the centre aisle of the bus, yelling, 'Mitchell, man, that's my book! What you do that for, you idiot?'

Mr Brownlow stood up. 'Mitchell and Kyle, come and sit here at the front with me please.'

Kyle grabbed his bag and climbed over Mitchell, grinning at us and storming to the front. Mitchell, gathering his bag and coat, whispered, 'Text me,' in my ear then strutted after Kyle to the front.

The coach drove down the side of Trafalgar Square and, as Nelson's Column and the lions came into view, everyone cheered. The coach stopped and everyone jumped up and gathered their coats and bags.

'You OK, Grace?' said Megan, squeezing my arm.

I nodded, but I felt sick to my toes.

We were last off the coach and kept our heads down as we passed Mr Brownlow.

'Hoods down, gentlemen, please,' he said, giving Megan's hood a tug.

The hood came down and all of Megan's curls fell out of the baseball cap.

Claude chose that moment to do a loud squeal.

Brownlow's mouth dropped open with horror.

22

Mitchell let out a roar and chased Kyle across the road. The pair of them jumped into the fountains and started punching each other. Several of the other boys jumped in to join them.

'You two girls, stay there!' Mr Brownlow shouted as he sprinted towards the fountain and jumped in to separate the boys.

'Now,' I yelled. Grabbing Megan's hand, we ran away from the fountains, past the National Gallery, up the side of the Portrait Gallery, on past Edith Cavell's statue and kept on running past the Coliseum. I stopped quickly to look around and spotted the best route.

'This way,' I said, pulling Megan across the

road. We kept on running past the Duke of York's Theatre and up to Freed's dance shop where Mum used to buy my tap shoes. I pulled Megan into Cecil Court, into a world of old bookshops and theatre stage doors.

I couldn't run any more. I bent double, a stabbing pain in my side. Megan was the same. She was leaning up against a wall, beads of sweat on her face. Fitting Claude's harness on, Megan lifted him out of the bag. He started to roll on the pavement.

A tall pretty dancer in a ballet dress was standing outside a stage door that was propped open. We could hear the laughter and applause of the audience. She was smoking a cigarette and stretching her legs against the wall. She looked at us with interest.

She poked her head back through the stage door.

'Come and look at this, Will,' she shouted. A tubby bald man came out.

'Well, look at that. Would the little fellow like some water?' he asked.

Megan nodded. Will the stage-doorkeeper disappeared and came back with a bowl of water and some apples. Claude tucked in, squealing with pleasure, then did a wee that trickled near the dancer's foot. She jumped out of the way, laughing.

'Sorry,' said Megan. 'He's busting – he couldn't hold it no more.'

'Don't worry!' the dancer said. 'I'm Harriet, by the way. It's my birthday today. Would you like some cake?' and before we could reply, she'd disappeared through the stage door and came back with two generous slabs of birthday cake wrapped in paper.

'Thank you, Harriet,' I said. 'If it's OK with you we'll eat those later. We've got to get going now.' I put the parcels in my carrier bag.

'What were you running from?' she asked.

'Running *to,*' I said. I thought quickly. 'We're meeting my mum at Leicester Square but we're late. We'd better go. Happy birthday, Harriet.'

And with that I lowered Claude back into the yellow bag and we ran through the end of Cecil

Court and out by Wyndham's Theatre and down the stairs of Leicester Square station to the ticket machine. Megan reached into the yellow bag for her purse. It had a hole chewed in the side and she pulled out half a five-pound note. Claude had eaten the rest of it.

'I've got money,' I said, reaching into the front pocket of my bag for the note that Mitchell had given me. But my purse had gone. It must have fallen out in the coach, or maybe when we were running. I started to panic. We were stuck and the police would be looking for us soon.

Just then a group of rowdy partygoers with streamers in their hair toppled down the station steps, drinking from beer bottles and popping party poppers.

'Follow me,' I whispered. I stood directly behind a girl with green hair and slipped through the barrier with her as she shoved her ticket in the slot and the gates opened. Catching on, a boy with blue hair beckoned to Megan to come through with him. The Underground man had not noticed, as an old lady was asking him directions.

'Have a nice night,' whooped the partygoers as they disappeared down the escalators, dancing and singing as they went. We took the long escalator to the Piccadilly line, followed the corridor round, then went down the steps.

Megan was gaping at everything. I propelled her to the end of the platform as she looked around at the posters and the people. The train pulled in almost immediately and we got in an empty carriage.

We let Claude out once the doors had shut and he started jumping from seat to seat to seat, squealing with joy. I started to laugh – a pig on the Piccadilly line! But I grabbed him before we reached Covent Garden. A snooty-looking lady in high heels and a black sparkly dress got on near us, stared at us in disgust, then got out again and into the next carriage.

'What's your problem?' shouted Megan.

The hoodies were coming in useful. No one else got on our carriage.

The stations started to speed by – Holborn, then Caledonian Road and Holloway Road. I felt a flutter in my tummy. I would soon be with Mum!

Wood Green, Arnos Grove. I started to smile.

Finally the train rolled into Southgate and the doors opened – and I could almost feel Mum's arms around me already. We jumped off the train, put Claude back in the yellow bag and started up the escalator.

There was one problem. No one else had got off. How were we going to get through the barriers on someone else's ticket this time? The station was deserted.

I threw myself on all fours and wriggled on my tummy underneath the ticket barrier. Megan passed Claude and our other bags over the top of the barrier, then threw herself on all fours too and started to wriggle under after me.

Just as I was getting up, a hand grabbed my shoulder.

'Come with me, sunshine,' said a voice.

23

I turned round to see a man with black hair, glasses and a big tummy, in a London Underground uniform. He had a name badge with *Gordon* on it. Megan scrambled to her feet. It was the first time I had ever seen her looking scared. He led us into a side office.

'Sit down,' he said. 'Travelling without a ticket is a criminal offence.'

I felt sick.

'I've just been radioed through to look for two young runaway girls fitting your description.' He reached for his notebook amongst the remnants of a half-eaten packed lunch on his desk. He found a pen under his sandwiches.

'Names and addresses,' he barked. In reply, a squeal rippled the air and Claude started struggling out of the bag on Megan's knee. She tried to grab him but he leaped on to the table and started rooting through the sandwiches and half-empty crisp packets. Gordon's mouth fell open and his face went beetroot.

'That's my dinner!' he roared, grabbing hold of a fish paste sandwich that Claude was gobbling. Claude bit him hard. Gordon started jumping up and down, waving his injured hand in the air.

'Run!' yelled Megan as she grabbed Claude. Snatching the bags, we belted out of the office, me leading the way. We sprinted down the high street, then right, then left, though the alley and up the small hill.

And then there it was: 22 Manderly Road. My home.

'Mum, Mum,' I yelled as I ran up the path and rang and rang the doorbell.

But she didn't answer the door. The house was in darkness. I rang the bell again. We waited. I peered through the letterbox. Silence. We crept down the passage at the side of my house. I stood on the bins and scrambled over the fence. Megan passed Claude to me and then leaped over the fence to join me.

I went to the third flower pot along, suddenly very glad that Mum kept a spare key – but it had gone. It started to rain.

Where was my mum? Lightning bolts of panic ripped through me.

Megan was peering up at the house and Claude was running up and down the garden, snorting.

'That window's slightly open,' Megan said. She was right – the bathroom window was slightly ajar. Megan started walking down to the bottom of the garden. 'Help me,' she called.

I hurried to join her. She was dragging a long plank of wood up towards the house. I grabbed the other end. A spider ran over my hand but I didn't let go even though they are my worst thing.

My useless, too-busy-for-me dad had been

going to make Mum a summer house with this wood but it had never happened. The wood still sat there, waiting.

We leaned the plank up against the house. It just reached the roof of the kitchen extension.

'Hold it still,' Megan said, and scrambled up it as easy as a cheetah up a tree. As I looked up, the rain stung my eyes. Megan pulled herself on to the kitchen roof and inched up its slope slowly, slowly. Her foot slipped on the wet slates and she started to slide down, but she grabbed a tile that was sticking out and managed to haul herself back up to the top again. Crawling sideways, Megan grasped the drainpipe and pulled herself up it to the bathroom window. Then she shoved it open and wriggled through.

I held my breath till the back door opened and she peered through the gap, grinning. I ran to her, my best friend in the world, and hugged her like I'd never let her go.

'Quick, take the wood back to the bottom of the garden,' she ordered. 'We don't want anyone to see. I'll get Claude.'

After we had chased him up and down the garden a few times, we caught him and crept through the back door. Megan put Claude down. He started running round the kitchen, snuffling.

'Mum,' I called. 'Mum!' But there was no answer. I ran up the stairs and pushed her bedroom door open, but the bed was empty.

I was suffocating under a landslide of disappointment and fear.

'Where is she?' I cried.

Megan grabbed hold of me. 'Don't panic,' she said. 'We'll find her. Maybe she's with a friend or something.'

'Something's wrong. I know it,' I said.

The answering machine on the phone was flashing: thirty-eight messages. My finger hovered over the button. Megan grabbed my hand.

'Don't,' she said. 'It will be them looking for us.'

I started to look through Mum's calendar that hung on the wall. By yesterday's date was a star and the word 'hospital' was circled in red.

'She must be still at the hospital,' I said. 'Something's gone wrong. We need to go there now.'

'Look, it's nine o'clock. I think it's too late,' said Megan, nodding at the kitchen clock. 'They won't let us in. We'll go there tomorrow. I reckon they just kept her in to rest, to stop her tiring herself doing the hoovering and polishing and things.'

As she spoke, Megan stood in front of the kitchen noticeboard. She pulled a letter off it and put it in her pocket.

'What's that?' I said.

'It's got the address of the hospital on it,' replied Megan.

'She's being treated at the Royal Warwick. It's where I had my appendix out. I know how to get there. It's near Goodge Street.'

'Even so,' said Megan. 'I'd rather have the address safe.'

I opened the fridge. Inside were a pint of milk, some lettuce, tomatoes and bacon.

'Cover Claude's eyes,' I ordered. Megan

grabbed hold of him and put a red tea-towel over his eyes. I took the bacon out of the fridge and, opening the freezer, I took out all the pork chops and sausages and took them outside to the dustbin.

'Oh well, I guess it's birthday cake for supper then,' said Megan.

The phone rang. Heart hammering, I reached out to answer it. Megan grabbed me, pinning my arms to my sides. The answer machine clicked into action and Grandad's voice rang out through the house.

'Grace, if you're there, pick up the phone . . . Pick up now, please. Grace, are you there? You're not in trouble. I just want you home with me here in Yorkshire. Please. Grace.' And then my grandad started to cry.

I struggled against Megan but she held me fast.

'Grace, come home. I am just a silly, foolish old man, who can't find the right words to talk to you . . . But I do love you, Grace. Megan, if you're there with our Grace, look after her.

Please. I will never stop you spending time together again. You have my word. You can run around the farmyard with yon pig to your hearts' content, just *please* come home.'

There was the click of Grandad replacing the receiver and the house was silent once more.

'Quick,' said Megan, springing into action, grabbing an empty plastic bottle from the recycling bag in the corner. She started filling it with tap water. 'We need to be ready to run when they come looking for us. We've got to keep warm. Grab a quilt or something. Hurry!'

I raced up the stairs to my bedroom and flung the door open. Purple curtains, carpet – purple everything – leaped out to meet me. It felt like a room belonging to another girl called Grace, not the Grace who dressed as a boy and got caught fare dodging on the Underground.

My dusty clarinet stood in the corner. My tap shoes peeped out from under the dressing table. I grabbed my purple quilt from the bed and raced out of the room. Dropping it on the landing, I ran back and pulled out my old turquoise comfort blanket that I kept secretly under the pillow and took my piggy bank from the shelf. Wrapping them in the quilt I started to drag everything downstairs.

Bang, bang, bang. The front door shook.

'Open up, please, it's the police.'

24

The door shook as a policeman banged on it.

'Megan, Grace, if you are there, open the door. We need to see you are both safe.'

Heavy footsteps shuffled on the gravel and radios crackled.

I froze halfway down the stairs.

'Go round to the neighbour, Gavin,' shouted one of the policemen. 'The grandfather said it's a Mrs Johnson.'

Megan appeared at the bottom of the stairs, clutching Claude and our bags.

'Quick,' she whispered. 'Out of the back door.'

We ran through the drizzle, tripping over the quilt as we went.

I looked up at Mrs Johnson's tree house, now covered with green summer leaves.

'This way,' I said, racing up to the fence between my garden and Mrs Johnson's. I found my top secret place, pushed open the fence's loose boards and we crawled through to the next-door garden, putting the boards back in place behind us.

We skidded down the slippery garden path to the big tree. I was praying over and over in my head that Mrs Johnson wouldn't look out of her window and see us. I started to shimmy up the rope ladder.

I reached the platform where the tree house was. Lying on my tummy, I stretched down to grab Claude from Megan, who was halfway up the ladder. She went down for the rest of the bags and I leaned over and grabbed them from her. Megan hauled herself up. We crawled into the tree house just in time as I saw two policemen walking out into my back garden.

We peered through the slats of the tree

house and watched the policemen walk round my garden, flicking on torches to help them search in the dusky light. I could see that one of the policemen was very tall with rosy cheeks and a big nose, and the other was short with a pointy chin and red hair.

'It's Grace and Megan who broke in all right, Gavin,' said the tall policeman. 'These are definitely pig prints. Look, there's some more in the flower bed.'

'Sir, over here,' shouted the short policeman, who must have been Gavin. 'Scuff marks on the fence. They climbed over the bins to get in.'

Mrs Johnson emerged from my back door just then and walked down the garden to join the policemen in the darkening night.

'Her quilt's gone off her bed and also her piggy bank from her shelf, but I don't think anything else of value's disappeared. Ah, the rain's stopped. At least they won't get drenched. I suppose that's a blessing. I found Grace's address book on her dressing table,' she said, handing my lemon-coloured address book to the tall policeman called 'Sir', who seemed to be in charge.

'We'll get on to it, see if they are staying with anyone. Who were her best friends at school?' he asked as he flicked through my private book.

'Jessica and a girl called Kayla, though I don't think they were very close towards the end. She'd come home from school upset. Left her out, they did. Oh, and she had a few friends at tap dancing, I think. They're all in the book,' said Mrs Johnson.

'Any spare keys anywhere?' said the one called Gavin.

'No, I took the ones kept under the flower pot into mine for safety.'

'They must have climbed through the bathroom window; that would have taken some doing,' said Sir, looking up. 'Show her the purse, Gavin.'

Policeman Gavin took my purple purse out of his pocket and showed it to Mrs Johnson. It was wrapped in plastic.

'This was sent by courier from the head of Brunswick Boys' School. It was found on the coach.'

Mrs Johnson nodded. 'It's Grace's – I bought it for her as a leaving present. Oh, where are they, officer?' Her voice was cracking.

'We are doing our very best, Mrs Johnson,' said the tall one called Sir. 'Two young lads, a Tyler Maison and a Zack Cudwell, were found asleep in the engine of a train at the Railway Museum in York.'

'Said they were running away to become famous footballers,' laughed Gavin. 'It's believed Megan and Grace travelled down to London in their coach dressed as the boys – and hiding a pig. The boys had pictures of the pig on their mobiles.'

'There have also been sightings in London. A stage-doorkeeper by the name of Will spoke to them, and a guard at Southgate station claims that a pig bit him and stole his crisps, and the two young girls he'd been holding for fare dodging ran away.'

'Grace wouldn't do that,' said Mrs Johnson.

I felt ashamed.

'When people don't have money, Mrs Johnson, they are pushed to all sorts,' said Sir. 'Grace's father is on board a flight to New Zealand on his way to a business conference. We've arranged for the New Zealand police to tell him when he lands. The grandfather has begged us not to tell her mother till tomorrow as she has had a bad reaction to her chemotherapy.'

'Yes, her temperature is very high. They've kept her in the Royal Warwick for the night. He's worried what this news might do to her,' said Mrs Johnson.

I felt as if I was falling out of the tree. Chemotherapy is what they give people for cancer. The scary words that had appeared on the computer screen when I had first Googled 'lump' danced into my brain and they stayed there. *My mum has cancer.* Now the thought had been thought out loud it could never be undone. My world smashed into smithereens.

Mitchell's mum, Sofia, had died of cancer. I curled up in a little ball and started rocking. I wanted to scream but Megan had hold of me tightly. Then everything happened at once.

The policemen's radios crackled into action, calling them to a raid on a jewellery shop. I let out a sob. Claude let out a tiny squeal. Mrs Johnson's eyes shot up to the tree house. As the police started running out of the garden, Gavin shouted, 'Phone the station straight away if they come back to the house.'

Now alone, Mrs Johnson came to the fence and shouted up to the tree house, 'Grace, are you there, love? Come down, please. I've been worried sick.'

Megan put her finger over her lips and scratched Claude's tummy with the other hand.

'I am too old to climb up and get you. If you are there, *please* come down.'

There was silence as Mrs Johnson just stood, looking up at the tree.

'Oh, well. I guess it was my imagination but, Grace, if you are there, if you are both there, I am sleeping in your mum's bed tonight at the front of the house, so I will hear if you come home. I'll make you something nice and warm to eat and one of my special hot chocolates. *Please* come home.' She shuffled back into my house.

Megan looked at me as she took Mitchell's too-big-for-her trainers and socks off her feet and started rubbing her red-raw toes.

'Give me the letter,' I said.

'What letter?' asked Megan.

'The letter you took off my mum's noticeboard,' I said.

Megan fished the crumpled paper out of her pocket. I smoothed it out and read it. It was an appointment booked for yesterday for my mum for a session of chemotherapy, starting at ten o'clock in the morning.

'You knew,' I said, tears pouring down my cheeks. 'How long have you known? Is that why you wanted to be friends with me before you even knew me, 'cause you felt sorry for me, just like the Easter egg people? You didn't *want* to be my friend. You just felt sorry for me 'cause my mum's got cancer.

 '*I hate you.*'

25

Megan looked at me, her face red and blotchy with anger. 'If you hate me then I'm going. I didn't *have* to run away with you, yer know. I did it 'cause we're blood sisters. I thought you were my best friend in the whole world. My only friend. Anyway, me and Claude have got better things to do than run round London after some mad girl carrying a bag of Easter eggs and making sure she doesn't get in some stranger's car, and end up dead on the front page of newspapers. Goodbye,' said Megan.

'You can't go,' I yelled. 'I won't let you.' I threw her trainers over the side of the tree house into the darkening night and then grabbed her wellies from the yellow bag and flung them too. They bounced through the branches on to the wet grass below.

'You silly cow, Grace,' shouted Megan. 'You can't stop me. I'll wear my new shoes. Forgot about those, didn't you?' She reached to the bottom of her yellow bag and pulled out a broken bit of strap, then a buckle, then a bit of rubber sole. We stared gobsmacked at the ruined shoes and then Megan began to laugh and laugh and laugh and my tears of sadness became tears of madness and we rolled around on the floor of the tree house howling, with Claude jumping on top of us, squealing. It was a good thing Mrs Johnson was sleeping at the front of the house.

'Claude, you clever boy,' laughed Megan. 'You knew I hated those shoes, didn't you?' Claude snorted and we started laughing all over again.

When we stopped Megan hugged me. 'Yes, I knew, and me mam knew too. She prays every night for your mam, 'cause she misses her so much, she said, it hurts. And, yes, she told me to be kind to you. But from the moment I saw you and watched your face from my window as your dad drove away and I saw you standing there alone with your grandad, I knew I wanted to be your friend. I wanted to be your friend more than anything in the world. I made a promise that Claude and I were going to make sure you were all right. He's your guardian angel pig.' She lifted him on to my knee and he buried his snout into my cheek.

'Why did no one tell me the whole truth – going on about little operations? It's all lies! They should have told me. I am ten years and twelve weeks and four days old,' I said.

'Truths from now on, blood sister. I vow to you,' said Megan.

'Truths,' I said, and Megan touched her hand to my elbow and gave me a kiss on the cheek. 'I'm so sorry,' she said.

'Mitchell's mum died,' I sobbed. 'I don't want my mum to die.'

'Grace, lots of people get better from cancer, me mam told me so. And that chemo's going to make sure all the nasty cancer cells have gone. We'll go to the hospital tomorrow and you'll see.'

'We'll give her the chocolate,' I said. 'Make her feel better.'

'Yes, the chocolate will definitely make her feel better,' said Megan.

I climbed down the rope ladder, holding the torch from the wellington boot cupboard in my teeth, to get Megan's wellies and trainers back from the garden.

I found one wellie by the fish pond, a trainer in Mrs Johnson's vegetable patch, and the other wellie in her rose garden. As I reached for it, I jumped as a pair of yellow eyes flashed back at me. It was the mangy fox that was always hanging around. It scurried away to the bottom of the garden.

I ran back to the tree to look for the other trainer. Suddenly light flooded the garden. I flung myself down in the shadow, clicking my torch off. The light was coming from my bedroom window. Mrs Johnson was looking out, dressed in her nightie. Her grey hair looked like an angel's halo in the light. She was staring up at the tree house. She looked sad. The garden went dark as she closed the curtain. I gave up on the other trainer and climbed the ladder.

Megan was preparing our supper. I realized we hadn't eaten all day. I grabbed the carrier bag of Easter eggs.

'No, we might need those,' said Megan.

My cheese and pickle sandwiches and Megan's jam ones from our packed lunches were all squashed. They looked and tasted disgusting, but we were too hungry to care. Claude helped us finish them.

Megan fished out the dancer's birthday cake from the carrier bag, handed me a piece and wrapped the quilt round us with Claude in the middle. We fed him bits of cake and shared the water. We used my jacket and Megan's red coat as a pillow and wrapped the extra jumper I had packed in my rucksack round Claude. Megan kissed me goodnight on the cheek.

'Best friends forever,' said Megan.

'Blood sisters till we die,' I said.

Megan and Claude fell asleep, but I didn't. I found my Special Blue Book and a pen in my purple rucksack and hugged my old turquoise comfort blanket to me and by torchlight I started to write.

TOMORROW I HAVE TO FIND MY MUM.

I will give her the Quality Street Easter egg with her favourite strawberry creams to help her feel better. I WILL NOT EAT ANY OF THEM. MUM CAN HAVE THEM ALL. We must get up really early and get to the hospital before Mrs Johnson, the police, Grandad or Miss Sams do. I AM FEELING REALLY HUNGRY AND SLEE—

26

I woke up with Claude's snout in my face. I was stiff and cold. I peeped out of the tree house. I heard our front door close. I crawled out on to the platform of the tree house and, standing on tiptoe, saw Mrs Johnson going down our front path with her shopping trolley. She was hurrying down the road.

I shook Megan awake.

'We've got to be quick. Mrs Johnson's gone to the shop. We need to leave now.'

'We should put on different clothes,' said Megan. 'They will be looking for our hoodies.'

I eased out my mum's dresses from my rucksack. I hesitated, then gave the pink one to Megan. She would fill it better than me. She had little bumps starting to show on her chest.

We pulled the dresses on. The pink one was very long on Megan but she looked so pretty. I was glad I had let her wear Mum's dress.

I emptied my piggy bank into my hand. I had ten pound coins, plus a few tens and pennies. We stuffed the money in the front pocket of my rucksack. I wrapped up my Special Blue Book and pen in the turquoise comfort blanket and shoved them in the rucksack too with our lunch boxes and the water bottles. We rolled up the hoodies in the quilt and left them in the corner of the tree house, before climbing down.

'Wait,' I reached into the carrier bag and chose a nice Easter egg filled with fudge. I tore out a page from my Special Blue Book and wrote:

Dear Mrs Johnson,

Thank you for the beautiful purple rucksack and suitcase. I am sorry I lost the purse and that I made you worry yourself sick.

I love you.

Grace XXX

I left it at her back door and we crawled through my top secret place and back into my garden. Megan scrambled over the fence on to the bins, I handed Claude to her, and then she helped me scramble over with all the bags. We started walking to Southgate station.

Passersby looked at the girl with the wild curls in the long pink dress and wellies carrying the yellow bag, and me, the girl with the short scraggy hair in the yellow dress. With every step my heart jigged harder against my ribcage as I prayed that no one would recognize us as the two runaway hoodies with the pig.

As Southgate station came in sight, I pulled Megan into an alley at the side of a newsagent's.

'We should go in separately, in case anyone recognizes us,' I said. Giving her some pound coins, I gave my instructions.

'Buy a single child ticket to Goodge Street. Make sure it's not that Gordon behind the ticket window. He'll be moaning on about his crisps again.'

Megan laughed, but I could tell she was scared.

'Then go down the escalator and I will meet you right at the end of the southbound platform,' I finished.

I watched her go. I could see her peep to see who was behind the ticket window. She ran over to the ticket machines, so it must have been Gordon. I saw a lady in a red raincoat show Megan where to slot the money in to get her ticket and then Megan disappeared down the escalator with a wriggling yellow bag.

I ran past the ticket window and, following the instructions on the touch screen of the machine, pushed in my pound coins and grabbed the ticket to Goodge Street that the machine spat out at me. I raced down the escalator, nearly falling as I went. A man in a brown suit grabbed my arm and said, 'Steady now. What's the rush?' But I raced by him to the bottom.

I saw Megan at the end of the crowded platform leaning over Claude in the bag and scratching his chin. A train pulled into the platform. I pushed through grumbling people to reach Megan and pulled her on to the train.

We plonked ourselves on two seats at the end of the carriage. I stood up, to let an old lady with a walking stick sit down, and clung on to the bar next to Megan's seat to keep steady. The old lady got out a bag of humbugs and rustled the paper bag as she offered one to Megan and me. Claude stuck his snout out of the bag. 'Good doggie,' she said, giving his nose a pat. I don't think her eyes were very good.

The train jogged and jolted us far too slowly through all the stations to Leicester Square. Nearer and nearer to my mum's hospital bed.

Pushing through the crowds, we followed the arrows to the Northern line and hopped on to the train to Goodge Street.

Only two more stops.

We climbed the stairs to the lift at Goodge Street and pushed our way in just as the doors were closing. In the lift, Megan took Claude out of the bag and put the harness on, much to the joy of a party of German school children and their blonde curly-haired teacher, who scratched Claude under his chin.

Megan and I were pushing our tickets into the barriers in the station foyer, but Claude had already spied the fruit stall outside. He dragged Megan through the gates and out of the station, and started guzzling an apple that had fallen on to the pavement.

'I'm so sorry,' said Megan. 'How much do you want for the apple?'

The dark-haired, stocky stall man started to chuckle and said, 'Don't worry about it, love.' He patted Claude and smiled, giving us each an apple. We grinned back to say thank you and put the apples in my carrier bag to give to Claude later.

I looked around, to work out the way to the hospital. I found some signs that led us through a concrete clearing and on to a path with trees. We followed the road round. There, in front of us, was the Royal Warwick Hospital.

'I'll wait here for you,' said Megan, pushing me forward. 'They won't let a pig in hospital.'

'You won't,' I said. 'My mum will want to meet you. You're Allie's daughter. She'll want you there with me.'

I unwrapped my Special Blue Book from my turquoise comfort blanket and put it in my rucksack. Then I picked up Claude, took off his harness, and wrapped him in the blanket like a newborn baby, handing him back to Megan. She grinned at me. I picked up all the bags and followed her into the hospital foyer. A lady in a blue skirt and stripy shirt made a soppy face and bent over to coo at the baby in Megan's arms, then recoiled in horror.

I walked up to a lady in glasses on Reception who was chatting on the phone about her holiday in Barcelona.

''Scuse me,' I said loudly. 'Sorry to disturb you, but my mum, Chloe Wilson, was kept in last night and I need to give these clothes to her so that she can come home.' I waved the bags at the lady.

The receptionist tutted and tapped something into her computer. 'She's in the Darwin Ward, eighth floor,' she said, and then carried on chatting about Barcelona.

We got into an empty lift. Claude had fallen asleep with his head against Megan's shoulder, snuggling his snout into my mum's pink dress.

The red lights flashed 2 . . . 3 . . . 4 . . . 5 . . . 6 . . . 7 and finally opened at 8. As we stepped out, following the arrows to Darwin, I felt sick to my toes. What would Mum say? Would she even be able to talk to us? Would she be too ill?

Taking a deep breath, I walked through the double doors, Megan by my side. We slipped past a side room where two nurses had their backs to us. There were lots of ladies sitting up in bed looking in mirrors and combing their hair. They were calling out, 'Lance,' to a man in tight jeans and a shocking pink shirt who was flitting from bed to bed telling the ladies how pretty they looked. There were a few nurses fiddling with various machines by the patients' beds.

At the end of the ward was a lady with a very pale face wearing a red scarf round her head. There was a wig on a polystyrene head on the cabinet beside her bed. She was lying back on the pillow with her eyes shut and she had a tube coming out of her arm. She had no hair.

It was my mum.

All her curls were gone, but it was her.

27

'Mum,' I called. 'Mum. Open your eyes. It's me, Grace.' I leaned over and kissed her. Mum's eyes opened. Almost all her eyelashes were gone.

'Grace,' she said. 'Grace, is it really you? How are . . . ? Why . . . ?' Her eyes flicked from joy to sorrow in less than a blink.

'Oh Grace, I didn't want you to see me looking like this.'

'Hug you, Mum,' I said. 'Hug you.' I held out my arms to her. She tried to do a 'Hug you more,' but she couldn't quite do it because she wasn't strong enough and because of the tube in her arm. So I bent down to give her my own special 'Hug you'. The tube got in the way and she smelled of hospitals, but I did the very best 'Hug you' I could.

'Where's your grandad, Grace?'

I swallowed. 'Grandad doesn't know we're here, Mum. We ran away.'

'You what?' she said and it was like a lightning bolt of strength shot through her as she struggled to sit upright in her bed. 'But why? Anything could have happened to you. Your grandad must be worried sick. How could you, Grace?'

'I wanted to give you this,' I said and I pulled out the Quality Street egg from the carrier bag and handed it to her.

'We thought it would make you feel better,' said Megan.

I turned round. Megan had a teardrop running down her cheek. I swallowed and swallowed, forcing my own tears jamming the back of my tonsils back down. I did not want to make Mum sad.

'You're Allie's Megan, aren't you? You're the image of her. Come here.' Mum held out her hand to Megan, who walked up to the bed. Mum smiled. 'You're wearing my old dresses! You both look lovely in them.'

With a squeal, Claude suddenly leaped out of Megan's arms, knocking the wig on the bedside cabinet into the air. It landed perfectly on Claude's head and he leaped away, running up and down the ward.

Lance the hairdresser started chasing Claude and screaming, 'My beautiful wig! Bring it back, piggy, right now!'

Megan and I were cracking up as we chased after Lance, trying to grab hold of Claude. Up and down the ward we went.

All the ladies in the beds, who I realized were also wearing wigs, started screaming with laughter. Soon the nurses were too. Then a lady in flowery overalls pushed a tea trolley through the doors at the end of the ward. Claude jumped over the bottom shelf of her trolley, knocking over the milk and grabbing a bun in his mouth in the process.

The tea lady ran up and down the ward

pushing her trolley and screaming, 'Help! Help! There's a wild animal in here!'

By this time, the ladies in the beds were laughing so hard their faces were bright red.

Then, in amongst everything, the two policemen from yesterday, Sir and Gavin, walked in and Sir slipped in the puddle of milk. He landed on his bottom and Gavin started to laugh so hard he couldn't help him up. Megan was just going over to help him when the doors at the other end of the ward swung open and in strode Grandad, followed by Allie, who was clutching a bag.

Grandad swooped down and caught the squealing Claude with one arm and removed the wig. Lance snatched the wig from Grandad and started to comb the tangles immediately. Grandad grabbed me with the other arm and hugged me so hard I couldn't breathe. And Allie burst into tears, hugged us both, then shouted, 'Do you know how worried we've all been? How could you!'

Then a doctor walked in bellowing, 'What's

going on in my ward? And will someone clean that milk up?'

But the ladies and nurses and Gavin still couldn't stop laughing. I grabbed hold of Megan's hand as the doctor looked round with a thunder face, drinking in the chaos. Then Claude *oink*ed and the doctor spun round on his heel and strode towards Grandad. I clutched Megan's hand with all my strength. We were going to be in such big trouble.

'How did a pig get in here?' barked the doctor.

Gradually the laughing tinkled out and there was silence.

Then slowly, slowly, the doctor's mouth began to twitch and he started to laugh. 'Marvellous things, pigs,' he said, 'very intelligent. I used to breed them, you know.' And the doctor started scratching Claude under his chin. 'Do carry on laughing,' he said. 'It's the best cure for sickness I know.'

The laughter rose again as Megan, Allie, Grandad and I walked back up the ward towards Mum's bed.

She now had some colour in her cheeks and a big smile on her face. Allie ran the last few steps, dumped her bag on the floor and hugged my mum like she would never ever let her go.

Lance ran up to the bed. 'Ladies and gentlemen and . . . um, piggy – if you will just give me a moment I would like to transform Miss Chloe into a princess.' He drew the curtains round my mum's bed.

We all stood outside and waited.

Lance whisked the curtains open and I gasped. My mum's wig was exactly like my hair – short and scraggy. She looked so beautiful.

Lance handed me a brush.

'Miss Grace, if you would do the finishing touches?'

I climbed on the bed next to my mum and did my best thing in the world. I brushed my mum's hair.

'I always thought your hair was so pretty,' she said. I felt the tears start to itch behind my eyes but I swallowed them back.

Allie pulled Megan away. 'Give them some time, love,' she said. They walked out of the ward, followed by Grandad, who was holding Claude. Allie stopped the doctor and started to talk to him.

And I pulled the curtain around my mum's bed so we could be alone.

THE NEXT BIT IS PRIVATE . . .

A VERY, VERY PRIVATE PART FROM MY SPECIAL
BLUE BOOK. I WILL ONLY LET YOU PEEP AT BITS
OF IT.

I held my head up high, looked Mum straight in the
eyes, and said, 'YOU SHOULD HAVE TOLD ME THE
TRUTH, MUM. I am ten years and twelve weeks and
five days. I am not a baby.'

Mum said, 'I'm sorry, Grace. You're right. I should
have told you.' She started to cry, so I snuggled up on
the bed next to her.

Mum told me at night, when her dreams came, she
was running round the farmyard with Allie, dancing and
laughing in wellies by the outside bog, behind the pig
pen, around the cowshed.

'I saw you, Mum,' I said, 'when I missed you most
– in shadows and in smoke and in the dazzling rainbow
light. But I'd go to hug you and you were never there.'

'I am here now,' she said, and she hugged me tight.

Then I told her about my dreams. How I'd listened
at doors and to telephone conversations and tried to

PRETEND TO MYSELF that she had got her lump when she'd knocked herself dancing. But when I was sleeping, my dreams had stuck all the bits of conversations I had heard together into a nightmare world which was far more frightening than the truth.

And that now I knew the truth we could plan together the best way to help her get strong again.

Mum said she was so sorry and she wished with all her heart that she'd told me that her lump was cancer.

Mum showed me the place on her breast and under her arm where the doctor had cut and I COULDN'T SWALLOW MY TEARS ANY MORE. THEY PINGED OUT OF MY EYES.

28

Allie peeped round the curtain and said that she needed to borrow me. She took me into a side office where Grandad, Megan, Claude and the two policemen, Gavin and Sir, were waiting.

Sir started to give us a stranger-danger lecture on the terrible things that can happen when you run away. A policewoman called Sandra slipped into the chair next to me and held my hand throughout the lecture. Allie kept butting in with: 'Yes, you tell 'em, officer.'

I tried to do my *blah blah blah* face but inside I felt sick. We'd made a lot of people cry – Miss Sams and Grandad and Mrs Johnson and Allie.

At the end of the lecture, Sandra whispered in my ear, 'She'll be all right, your mum, you know. Now you're together again.'

Sir and Gavin shook Grandad's hand and left. We went back to the Darwin ward where the doctor was waiting by the bed, holding a bin.

Allie reached into her bag and brought out an old can of blue paint.

'Well, Chloe, are you going to keep your promise? Come and paint my door blue? I've waited long enough.'

'One day.' Mum laughed.

'No. Not one day. Now,' said Allie.

'I've had a word with Mrs Haggett here,' said the doctor, 'and we've come to an arrangement. She's made a vow. Open your bag.'

Allie held it open. Inside were cigarette papers and tins of tobacco. The doctor held the bin open and Allie tipped them all in.

'I love you, Chloe Wilson – Chloe Bradley, that was – and I have promised never to smoke again and cause harm to myself and those around me that I love. You two are coming to live with me till you're better, or for as long as you want. When you've finished your chemotherapy and you have to start radio-therapy, the doctor here says that we can transfer you to the Middleton Hospital in Yorkshire.'

Megan whooped and flung her arms around me. She picked me up and whirled me round.

'I think it's a splendid idea,' said the doctor. 'With some good country air and a fine pig like Claude to keep you amused, we'll soon have you on your feet.'

'That's ridiculous,' blustered Grandad. 'I've never heard anything so daft. You can't all squash up in that tiny cottage when I'm rattling around in my huge farmhouse. Come and stay with me, Chloe – you and Grace.'

'Mr Bradley,' said Allie, 'your house is cold and draughty with lots of stairs and a mad dog who knocks everyone over. My cottage is cosy and snug and she needs me, a woman, to help her bath and dress on the days she's not feeling so good. You've parted us once and I will never let you separate me from our Chloe again.'

Grandad shrunk into a burst party balloon.

'Chloe, I lost you for eleven years with my foolishness once and I won't lose you and our Grace again. I misjudged you, Allie – and you too, Megan – and I hope you'll forgive an old man.'

'Course we do,' said Allie, softening. Megan kissed Grandad on the cheek. 'There will be plenty of room. Our Ryan is going to stop at Kylie's, and that husband of mine has promised to lay off the beer and be on his best behaviour so that the cottage is calm for our Chloe. And, Mr Bradley, you are welcome at our cottage for your tea whenever you want.'

'I hope you've got some paint brushes ready,' laughed Mum.

'That's settled then, splendid,' said the doctor. He shook Grandad's and Allie's hands, patted Claude, and strode out of the ward.

'I guess you should all stay at ours tonight,' said Mum, reaching into her bedside locker and handing Grandad our front door keys.

'There are pork chops in the freezer that you can have for your tea.'

'Mum!' I said, covering Claude's ears, who was now sitting on her bed. 'Pork chops and mash is not my best meal any more, it's my worst. Anyway, we've got plenty to eat here.'

I tipped all the remaining Easter eggs out on the bed. Megan and I broke the chocolate into bits and handed pieces round to all the ladies in wigs in the beds, to the nurses, and to Allie, Mum and Grandad, and we all started to eat. Mum tucked in to her Quality Street egg. I could tell she felt better.

'What's your best meal now then?' asked Mum.

'Chocolate,' I whispered.

THE LAST PRIVATE PART OF MY SPECIAL BLUE BOOK
THAT I WILL LET YOU PEEP AT.

I am looking out of the cottage window and Grandad
is walking towards the cottage with a big bunch of
flowers in one arm and a baby black pot-bellied pig in
the other. He is smiling like it's not too much effort for
his lips and his eyes are twinkling again.

I'm putting down this book to run to open the
BRIGHT BLUE door to Grandad . . .

I held my arms open and Grandad put the tiny pig
in them. He snuffled into my shoulder and I squirmed
with delight. He has blue eyes and is my best thing in
the world. I've called my pig Albert, which is Grandad's
first name. Grandad said he doesn't know whether to
be insulted or honoured that a little pest of a pig is
named after him. I think he likes it really. Albert is
even naughtier than Claude and chews everything.

Mum and I live here properly now. Before we
moved, Mum had to finish her chemotherapy sessions
in London. On those days, Allie went down to our house
in Southgate so she could look after Mum when she

came out of hospital and also to help Mrs Johnson do the housework.

When Allie went to London, Megan and Claude would stay at the farmhouse with me and Grandad.

Grandad made us sit at the dining room table and write letters to say we were sorry to:

Miss Sams

The headmaster of Brunswick Boys' School

The staff at the Railway Museum (Megan for pushing over the wax model of Queen Victoria, me for causing mayhem and distress – Grandad's words, not mine)

Will the stage-doorkeeper and Harriet the dancer (for telling them a fib)

Lance the hairdresser

– and the hospital tea lady (Beryl) who claims she still hasn't recovered from a pig stealing her buns.

(We didn't tell Grandad about Gordon at Southgate station. We thought a pig-bite and stolen crisps would mean a very long letter – and our arms already ached.)

Mum's had some radiotherapy today which is why Grandad's come to tea to spend some time with her. Mum takes each day one step at a time and says that every moment in life is precious.

If this was some fairy story you were reading instead of my story, my dad would see the error of his ways and want to come back to me and Mum. Well, he didn't. I haven't seen him since he drove away. Apparently he's met some lady in New Zealand, but I don't care too much 'coz I've got my grandad, who's never too busy for me.

You are probably wondering if I texted Mitchell.

Well I did and his dad Leon has brought him up several times to visit 'for some good country air and some mothering', as he puts it.

They sleep at Grandad's.

And Mitchell's Aunty Allie and Aunty Chloe can't do enough for him. Fight over him, they do. It makes Megan and me laugh.

Leon's kind, like Mitchell, and they look very alike. He has one of those posh cars with a roof that goes down – like Lucy Potts's, only better. When we drive past Lucy's, Megan and I STICK OUR HANDS OUT AND WAVE LIKE THE QUEEN.

Leon says he can't wait to see Mum's hair ruffling in the breeze when her curls start to grow again. He always helps her tie a bandanna round her head. He takes us on trips to Longleat and Haworth, and the Lake District. He calls us his ladies.

Mitchell won't come on the trips. He says, 'History trips have got me in enough trouble, thank you very much,' and stays with Grandad on the farm to help him milk the cows. Grandad's taken a proper shine to Mitchell; he says it's nice to have a boy about the place after all the squealing women and pigs giving him a headache.

Mitchell did come to York with us though, back to the Railway Museum, and we all went on the steam train together.

Oh yes, and one of the best things was when we all went on a trip to London to the theatre. When they got our letters, Harriet and Will sent us lots of free tickets to their show. Harriet was dancing the lead role that night and we were allowed into her dressing room afterwards. After she had met Mum and Allie she threw her cigarettes in the bin, held Allie's hand and joined in her vow to stop smoking.

Grandad has planted a weeping willow tree for Mitchell's mum, Sofia, in the farmyard. We had a special ceremony and tea afterwards.

And I've realized that sometimes family isn't the one you are born into, but the people and pigs you collect along the way.

Megan and I and Mum and Allie and Claude and Albert go for walks in the evening. We play and dance and laugh in wellies by the outside bog, behind the pig pen, and around the cowshed, and always stop at Sofia's tree before going back through the door that is now bright blue.

Acknowledgements

I would like to thank my amazing agent, Jodie Hodges, for her wisdom and belief and for keeping my feet firmly on the ground until my dream became a reality. Naomi Greenwood, my very special editor, who nourished *A Room Full of Chocolate* with her creativity and made each stage from my laptop to the bookshelf a joyful adventure. Everyone at Hodder, including Michelle Brackenborough for the gorgeous book cover and design.

A big thanks to Kaal Dewar for his computer genius, artistry and sheer patience, Clare Calder for her never-ending support, Sharon Marlow for her tap dancing expertise, Lou Kuenzler for her guidance and for leading me into the world of being a children's author through her workshop at City Lit. Also the Ladies of the Royal Festival Hall: without your feedback and support this would not have happened, and to Callum Calder and Addie Mitchell from Breast Cancer Care for your advice when researching.

Finally, I would like to thank Jenny Elson, Naomi Jones, Christopher Ryan and Marcia Mantack, my first readers who kept me going with their belief and Mo O'Hara for leading me on to the path to publication.

In honour of Claude, of course I can't forget the animals who inspired my story: Justy and Wendy the golden retrievers who shared my childhood, Griffid my late beloved blind ginger cat and Larry my retired one-eyed alley cat for keeping me company during the endless joyful hours of writing *A Room Full of Chocolate*.

Discussion Points

- *A Room Full of Chocolate* tackles a number of themes: *Friendship, Family, Illness, Bullying, Communication, Secrets, Fears*

  Can you think of an example of where the story touches on each of these themes?

- What makes a good friend?

- How do we rely on friends to give us what grown-ups/parents can't?

- There are different methods of communication and different types of narrative in the book – e.g. straight narrative; diary; text messages; notes; Grace and her mum's code. What does it add to the book? How do people use different types of communication for different things?

- There are many secrets in this book. Why do people keep secrets? When is it right to keep a secret and when is it wrong to keep a secret?

- Sometimes adults get things wrong – can you think of times in the book when adults should have perhaps acted differently? How should they have acted instead?

Praise for
How to Fly with Broken Wings

'An absorbing, well-crafted read full of surprises ... you may need to keep tissues handy' *Primary Times*

'This book tugged at every single one of my heart strings ... a truly mesmerising read that will have you shouting at the page and re-evaluating how you look at/treat people you come across in daily life' *Bibliobeth.com*

'The writing is elegant and flowing and the observation of the teen and tween mindset is spot on' *The Bookbag*

'... a story that will both break you and rebuild, ground you, yet make you fly! A perfect addition to any library (or home)' *Readingzone*

TURN THE PAGE TO READ
AN EXTRACT ...

1

WILLEM

When Finn Mason shouts 'jump', you jump as high as you can or you are dead.

I took a deep breath.

'Jump, you muppet,' yelled Finn, a dot of spit escaping from the corner of his mouth.

TJ and Laurence stood either side of him. They were staring up at me. Their mouths were open.

I inched my toes forward over the edge of the school wall. A bit of the broken glass that Mr Patricks, our school caretaker, had spread along the top to keep us *in* school and burglars *out* of school, scrunched under my feet. No burglars would ever want to come into our school because there is nothing left to steal. Finn Mason has stolen everything already.

'Jump! Jump! Jump!' chanted Laurence and TJ. Laurence was laughing. TJ looked as if he was about to be sick. My fingers started to jiggle.

I reached into my right pocket for my model of a Spitfire Mark 1.

It had gone! Spinning the propeller calms my hands and helps me focus on solving difficult problems, for example this one where I am being forced to jump off a very high wall. I pushed my hand into my left pocket even though it is a fact that I always keep my model Spitfire Mark 1 in my right pocket. It was not there. It was lost. My fingers jiggled faster.

I should not have been on top of the school wall. I should have been doing my homework. Mrs Hubert, my Maths teacher had given me different homework from the rest of the class. They had to complete 10 equations.

I had to make 2 friends.

Mrs Hubert said that my gran does not count because she is a relative. Bernie from Bernie's Burger Bar does not count because he is a shopkeeper. I asked Mrs Hubert if she was my friend and she said no, she is my Maths teacher.

'You must make 2 friends your own age,' she said.

'Jump!' screamed Finn.

He is not my friend.

I inched a bit further forward.

A piece of glass went through the thin bit at the bottom of my left, black, second-favourite school lace-ups and cut into my big toe.

Mr Patricks should not put glass on top of the wall because of health and safety. Mr Patricks should not be a school caretaker. He should be an SAS assassin.

It's funny, isn't it, the things that go through your mind when you are about to jump off a wall and die?

An aeroplane droned above me. I looked up. I think it was a Boeing 747-400, but it is hard to tell when you are trying to balance on top of a very high wall. They can fly without stopping for up to 7,670 nautical miles. Aeroplane facts make me feel calm.

'Jump,' shouted Finn.

Finn has blond curls on his head. He does not comb his hair. He has 7 freckles on his nose. I counted them when he made me jump off my school desk yesterday at breaktime. Finn, TJ and Laurence looked very small from up on the wall.

'I said JUMP!' screamed Finn.

I looked down.

I, Willem Edward Smith, would like to state here to you that I am not afraid of heights. We live on the 18th floor of the Beckham Estate. 'We sleep higher than the birds,' says my gran. If I was about to die then I was going to ask whoever is in charge up there – say God or, if I couldn't get to see him, his assistant St Peter – if I could come back as a bird because I do not like being Willem Edward Smith very much.

My Gran says to *always go to the top*. So I hoped God was available for my request. Maybe I could make an appointment with him.

Another thing my Gran says is that *I must plan for everything* so that I don't get any nasty surprises in life. So whenever I see Finn walking down the school corridor I always start jumping up and down on the spot before he can tell me to. I ruffle my hair and pull a button off my shirt and smack myself in the face so I have a red mark on my cheek. My plan is that Finn will think he has beaten me up already.

Finn has a short attention span so sometimes this works, but other times he makes me jump higher and kicks me in the stomach.

'Jump! Jump! Jump!' they chanted louder and louder.

My fingers jiggled faster. Who would make Gran her morning cup of tea and bring her a plate of digestive biscuits if I died jumping off the school wall? Which, by the way, I thought would be a pitiful way to end my very short life of 12 years and I started to count the days, minutes and seconds I had been on Planet Earth.

'Jump, you pathetic piece of filth.' Finn interrupted my calculation.

I took another deep breath and inched my toes further over the edge. The ground started to spin. I wobbled. TJ put his hands over his eyes. A girl screamed.

Sasha Barton was running towards us.

'Finn, what are you doing? If you hurt him you'll be chucked out of school again and we won't see each other. Not ever. My dad will ban you from my life for the sixth time this year.'

Sasha looked up at me and did the tiniest of

winks. It was barely a flicker, but I saw it. If someone winks at you, does that mean that they are your friend? Then she flicked her long black hair behind her ears, shook her gold hoop earrings and flung her arms around Finn.

'Leave Willem alone, Finn, *please*,' she said, staring into his eyes.

Finn did not look into Sasha's eyes. He stared at her bumps. Except her bumps are not very big – not big enough to stop Finn wanting to kill me.

'JUMP!' he roared.

So I JUMPED. I pretended I was in a flying machine and I didn't mean to but I must have flapped my arms like a bird's wings on the way down and let out my secret, and as my foot went snap underneath me I screamed.

But I wasn't dead. I was still Willem Edward Smith who lived on the 18th floor, Flat 103 of the Beckham Estate, Beckham Street, North West London, NW1 7AD.

Finn started to laugh. Then they all started to laugh because Finn was laughing.

He bent close to me and hissed in my face, 'He thinks he's a frigging bird. Fly, boy, fly.'

'Oi! What do you lot think you're doing?' It was Mr Patricks the caretaker sprinting toward us.

'Run!' yelled Finn.

Finn grabbed Sasha's hand and they all ran away, leaving me on the ground with a foot that had snapped. Something glinted in the grass. It was Sasha's gold hoop earring. I reached out and grabbed it, even though it is a fact that you should not move after an accident. It hurt. I hid the earring in my pocket. It was evidence that Sasha was there when I jumped off the wall and I did not want someone who might be a friend getting into trouble.

'One day,' I shouted after them. 'One day I'll fly.'

Photograph © Paul Barrass

JANE ELSON

After performing as an actress and comedy improviser for many years, Jane fell into writing stories and plays. Her debut novel, *A Room Full of Chocolate*, was nominated for the Carnegie Medal and won Peters Book of the Year 2015 and the Leeds Book Award. When she is not writing Jane spends her time running creative writing and comedy improvisation workshops for children with special educational needs. She also enjoys volunteering at Kentish Town City Farm.

aroomfullofwords.com

🐦 @JJELSON35